# HER ALIEN BODYGUARD

## STRANDED ON EARTH: A PREQUEL

## IVY KNOX

Cover art: Natasha Snow Designs

Edited by: Tina's Editing Services, Chrisandra's Corrections, Mel Braxton Edits, & Owl Eyes Proofs & Edits

❀ Created with Vellum

# AUTHOR'S NOTE

If you don't have any concerns regarding content and how it may affect you, **feel free to skip ahead to avoid spoilers**!

This book contains scenes that reference or depict kidnapping, sexual harassment, eating disorders, fatphobia, ableism, gun violence, racism, sexism, neglected animals, as well as graphic violence, which may be triggering for some. If you or someone you know is in need of support, there are places you can go for help. I have listed some resources at the end of this book.

# CHAPTER 1

## LUKASSANAI "LUKA"

DATE: OCTOBER 20, 2007 LOCAL TIME: AROUND 11 P.M.

"They need to think we died," I shout into the mouthpiece inside my helmet as I rip the small circular discs from the side of my throat and behind my ears. "Disconnect your bio trackers. Now!"

"It is done," Axilssanai, my brother, confirms from inside his own escape pod.

"Done."

"Done."

My brothers Mylossanai and Zevssanai confirm simultaneously.

Just as I am about to release a torrent of Sufoian expletives on Kyanssanai—who is a constant source of frustration for the rest of us—he confirms his indicator is disconnected as well. Then he asks, "How long until impact?"

Axilssanai answers, "Ten ticks." His escape pod has an added set of screens to map our path toward Earth's surface. We have breached Earth's atmosphere and will soon crash.

I close my eyes, trying to bring the reasons for this treacherous journey to the forefront of my mind. Then I list them for the others to hear. Surely, as they brace for impact, they will need this reminder too. "We have come here for our freedom, brothers. To build a life that is entirely our own."

"Six ticks," Axilssanai interjects.

"There was nothing for us on Sufoi, nothing but emptiness," I add. "We are here to begin anew. To find our purpose."

"Four ticks."

"And most importantly, to find mates," I say with a pleased sigh. "Our handlers said they do not exist for us. They did not speak the truth. We shall find them here. I feel it in my blood."

"Ready yourselves for impact."

Axilssanai barely gets the words out before my body jerks forward against my safety straps and my shoulder slams into the hard metal of the door. Smoke clouds my vision as the stench of fuel and burning metal finds my nose. Blinding pain shoots down to my wrist as alarms blare inside my escape pod, and then…there is nothing. Blackness. The kind of black that feels cold and eternal.

Time passes. I do not know how much, but when my vision clears, I see the door of my pod being ripped off its hinges, and the faces of my brothers in their draxilio forms come into view as they use their sharp claws, teeth, and horns to rip away the safety straps and haul my body into the crisp night air. They pull my helmet off and set me on my feet as they shift back into their flightless forms.

As I shake the blurriness from my head, the scent of our new environment hits me. Beyond the burning metal, the air is surprisingly lovely. Tilting my head back, I see the tall trees with the sparse, spiky green leaves swaying in the wind, filling my lungs with a crisp, invigorating fragrance. It mingles with the richness of the newly exposed roots of the trees our pods knocked down in the crash.

"Are you certain this will work?" Zevssanai asks, his different-colored eyes nervously scanning the stars. "They will not follow us here?" Possessing the softest heart among us, Zevssanai was often the recipient of the cruelest acts of abuse by our handlers, or more accurately, our creators. They created us in a laboratory and monitored our every move until we were strong enough to serve as the king's personal assassins. I fear those memories will haunt Zevssanai for the rest of his days.

"No, they will not follow us here," I reassure him with a squeeze of his shoulder. "As far as anyone on Sufoi knows, we are dead. Our handlers were not even aware of our departure. They will learn of it, that is certain, but our ship exploded as we neared Earth's atmosphere, and our bio trackers lost their connection immediately after that, making it appear as if we did not survive—that our pods were still inside the ship at the time the bombs detonated. There would be no reason for them to follow our path."

Zevssanai's eyes meet mine, and he dips his chin, his cerulean skin paling a bit. It is as if he is desperately wishing he could believe me, but years of conditioning by our handlers keeps him firmly planted in a state of worry.

"What now?" Kyanssanai asks, placing his hands on his narrow hips and letting out an exhausted huff. "Where are we?"

Axilssanai's heavy gait vibrates the ground as he stomps toward us. "We have landed in a stretch of forest within a place called, uh," he pauses, looking at the map on his navigation watch. "Mass-ah-shoo-sits," he says slowly. "The closest urban area is called Baws-tonn, and we should come upon it in under forty ticks once we take to the skies. In that direction." He turns and points.

Mylossanai's eyes widen. "I have not heard of this country." He reaches for Axilssanai's wrist to see the map, but Axilssanai snatches it away. "Why have we not heard of such a place? We studied Earth's regions and the history of its people. The human history that we could access anyway." Then in a lower, condescending tone, he mumbles, "I did, at least."

Axilssanai grunts in annoyance. "Baws-tonn is the biggest urban area in Mass-ah-shoo-sits, which is in the northern part of the United States of America."

"Ah, America," Mylossanai exclaims with a relieved grin. "I am familiar with America. I did much historical reading on it. The ones who wore the buckles left the royals across the sea and took over this land centuries ago."

"That is it?" Kyanssanai scoffs. "That is all you learned about this place? What of the humans of today?"

Mylossanai's lips purse, his gaze drifting to each of us. "There are many countries on this planet, brother. I did not know where we would crash."

"Do they still have a fondness for the buckles?" Zevssanai asks, making a face that indicates he very much hopes the answer is no.

Mylossanai shrugs.

"I do not think I would look good covered in buckles," Kyanssanai adds, running a hand through his wavy hair.

"You definitely would not," Mylossanai adds in a biting tone.

Kyanssanai's calculated glare tells me he is eager to continue quarreling with Mylossanai, and could spend several *pivs* doing so, but we have much more pressing business to attend to, so I step forward and put up a hand. "Stellar information, brother," I tell Mylossanai. "But we must melt these pods and make our way toward Baws-tonn. Remember? We created a very clear plan we must stick to. Destroy the pods, fly over the urban section, and scan the faces of humans to determine the best shade to mask our blue skin."

My brothers nod in unison, shifting into our draxilios as we turn toward the escape pods. A short inhale is all we need to complete this job, and within half a tick, our pods become puddles of molten steel amid the smattering of dried orange and red leaves that cover the ground.

There is a calmness that washes over every draxilio from being able to use our fire. The act of it strengthens the bond between the two beings who share the same body—the males we are in this form and the feral, winged beasts capable of turning the world to ash.

*Right. Onward toward Baws-tonn,* I send my brothers through the mental link we share in draxilio form. Concurring grunts follow my command, and the moment we lift our clawed feet off the ground, we cloak our large bodies, making ourselves invisible to any human onlookers below.

We pass over clumps of houses huddled together on darkened streets. The sounds of small animals racing across tree branches meet my ears, but there are no human noises to be heard. There does not seem to be much activity at this time in the sparsely populated areas beyond Baws-tonn. But once we find a wide path with a line of automobiles, we follow it until the steady hum of human voices begins to grow.

We fly over a structure that is shaped like a giant distorted bowl, open to the sky, but closed on all sides, filled with almost deafening human shouts and cheers. In the center of this bowl is a stretch of vibrant green grass with an outline of dirt forming a diamond shape. On one side of the bowl is a vast green wall, a few shades darker than the grass. I cannot tell what this place is, but the humans inside are wearing red and white and seem quite pleased to be there.

*There are many pale faces here,* Kyanssanai notes when he reaches a strip of roadway with several bustling businesses. *No buckles, however.*

*Kov, that is what I see as well,* Zevssanai adds in agreement.

*Let us spread ourselves wide to be sure,* I caution them. If Earth is anything like Sufoi, there will be sections of the urban areas where certain groups of beings congregate. We cannot choose our shade based on a small cluster of pale faces.

Once we begin settling into our lives among the humans, we will need to create new identities with the applicable documents humans use. Choosing the shade of skin to mask ourselves with is not something that can be undone. We must get it right the first time.

While the genetic modifications we were given at birth by our handlers allow us to change our skin to any color at any given time, we do not wish to change our appearance multiple times during our time on this planet. That kind of behavior would surely be seen as suspicious, and the last thing we can afford to do is raise suspicions. We aim to have quiet, simple lives here and not gain the attention of the local patrollers.

Axilssanai lets out an amused grunt. *There appears to be something happening over here.*

Flapping my wings, I glide through the clouds until I reach his side. When I do, I notice a group of humans exiting a large structure, flooding out onto the street. They seem quite jovial in spirit. Many of them stumble a bit as they make their way onto the sidewalk, and all of them are the very shade of pale that we have been seeing since we crashed.

*Let us choose that pale shade,* Axilssanai sends, gesturing to the crowd below. *We can hide in a crowd that size, especially if our skin is the same.*

*Do you not think it is a bit early to determine our shade?* I ask hesitantly.

Kyanssanai scoffs. *Have you tripped over your own tail? I am sick of watching from above. Let us start our lives. If it is the wrong shade, we will change it before we obtain our official identities.*

*Our mates could be in that crowd,* Mylossanai points out.

He is right, and that removes my reluctance entirely. *Let us descend.*

We follow Axilssanai to the alley behind the building we have been watching and shift into our flightless forms the moment we land next to a foul-smelling waste receptacle. I revel in the feeling of my bones shrinking and my wings folding in on themselves as I form this other body. It was terrifying as a child to shift back and forth between my two forms, but I find it calming now.

It is quite lucky that my brothers and I have clothing blocks implanted in our arms, otherwise, we would be caught in the nude after each shift. The clothing block senses the shift and removes our clothes before the shift is complete, and then puts them back on when we return to our flightless form. It is perhaps the one technological achievement our handlers on Sufoi got right.

One by one, we hide our horns and mask our blue skin with the pale shade we saw on the many faces filling the streets of Baws-tonn. We stare at each other in wonder for a tick, marveling at our new human look.

When we make our way to the front of the establishment, we are instantly lost in the crowd. We are the tallest beings here by far, which is not ideal. I did not realize how small most humans are. Sufoians are biologically capable of procreating with humans—something we made sure to verify—but the difference in size between us and the humans milling about around us is quite jarring. We do not blend in among this group of clumsy, pale faces, all of whom seem to be singing parts of different songs as they exit the large structure behind us.

My heart stops when a strong, intoxicating scent unfurls within my nostrils. It is sweet and rich, like the fruit syrup drenching a fresh batch of *nocavi* cakes. My head whips around in the direction of it, and my feet take me forward as I inhale deeply, desperate to hold it within my lungs. My pulse races, and a sheen of sweat covers my hands. It is *her*. My mate. It has to be. No other scent has ever had such a strong hold on me.

I push through the endless sea of humans, my nose as my compass, searching for a body, a face, to connect the scent to, but all the females I see have their arms wrapped around male companions. A gust of wind whips past me, lifting the ends of my hair, but it takes her magnificent scent with it. It is gone. No matter how deeply I breathe in, I can find it no longer.

Before I was able to see her face, she disappeared.

# CHAPTER 2

## LUKA

*I* am tempted to continue chasing the scent of my mate when a loud male voice breaks through the various others singing around me. When I turn toward it, I see my brothers standing together, eyeing me curiously. I cannot abandon them to search for some phantom female. They become chaotic menaces in my absence. I must see to us finding shelter for the night.

"Water, five dollars!" the male voice shouts. "Candy, three dollars!" He stands in front of the next building over from the doors the humans are piling out of.

"Good fellow, what is the reason for this crowd?" I ask, gesturing to the mass of bodies still filling the sidewalk.

"It's the Trippin' Billygoats. Their shows always sell out," he says, as if that is sufficient information. When I continue to stare blankly at him, he adds, "You know, the Dave Matthews tribute band?"

He eyes me with a hint of suspicion, which is the last thing I want. "Ah, yes. Of course," I reply, pretending to understand.

The man's brow furrows as he takes in our attire. "Are you guys basketball players? Or…strippers?"

I look down at the fitted, metallic silver jumpsuit I am wearing—what we all wear—and feel foolish for not realizing how out of place we look before now. No one wears anything like this. At least not in the crowd of Trippin' Billygoats supporters.

"No," I begin, adding a nervous chuckle that I hope will disarm him, "we are not from around these parts." Then a yellow and red stick on his small table catches my eye. "What do you have there?"

"That?" he asks, pointing to it. "Starburst. You've never had Starburst before?"

"No. What is it, exactly?"

He lets out an astonished gasp. "It's candy, bro. Here," he hands the colorful stick to me, "on the house."

Carefully, I pull open the bright wrapper and discover several colorful cubes inside with lettering on them. I pop two of the yellow cubes into my mouth and hand the rest to my brothers. "Hmm," I grunt as I chew, "it is sweet, but has quite a rough exterior, yes?"

The man covers his mouth in horror. "Yooo, did you eat the wrappers too?"

Embarrassed, I swallow slowly and nod. "Was I not supposed to?" I am failing miserably at this human act.

"Jesus, have you never eaten candy before?" The man's eyes dart between me and my brothers for a moment, then pity swirls in his dark-brown eyes when he notices the matching gold and emerald pendants around our necks. "Are you guys in a cult?"

Axilssanai steps forward. "Yes, we were in a cult. Our handlers were quite cruel, so we escaped." Then Axilssanai shoots me a subtle nod. My brother has always been gifted at reading people and reacting accordingly in the moment. I very much appreciate that about him.

The human man leans his body against the brick wall behind him. "Fucking handlers? You had handlers? Aw, shit. That sucks, man. Was it the same cult as the one with those red bracelets all the celebrities wear?"

I have no idea what he speaks of, but this cult farce seems to be working, so I continue it. If pity will urge this human to help us, I shall spin a tale of woe unlike any he has ever heard. "Not that one. But it was horrifying and oppressive. They tortured us. We were lucky to escape with our lives."

Something strange happens next. I begin to sense the man's heart-beat—strong and steady. I become attuned to the pace of his breathing, and when his eyes lift to meet mine, it is as if he becomes trapped inside my gaze. I do not know how, but I even feel the malleability of his brain in this state, causing me to wonder if I am meant to mold it in some way. It is soft and squishy—this man's brain. This has never occurred before, and I do not know what it means, but I decide to test the boundaries of this newfound control.

"We must find shelter and we require your assistance," I say, keeping my voice low, my newfound power tying a thread between my mind and his.

He stares at me for a moment, unmoving and as if in a trance, then nods and points to the building behind him. "You can stay with me. I'm Jay. I own this pawn shop, and my apartment is right above it. Follow me."

We enter through a brown door with chipped paint and follow him up a set of stairs so creaky beneath us that I wonder if we will fall through before we reach the top. Luckily, they remain sturdy as he leads us into his small, humble home. It appears to have only one door with the rest opening into a big room. There are stains from old leaks running along the ceiling and down the faded beige walls, wilting plants hang from the ceiling in front of large windows, and the bright yellow glare from his store's sign lights up his entire home.

"Bathroom's over there," he says in a robotic, even tone, pointing to the single door. "One of you can have the couch and the rest will have to sleep on the floor, but I'll grab some sleeping bags for you."

There will be no true sleeping this night, of course, as we cannot maintain our masks while asleep, and we cannot risk Jay seeing us with horns and blue skin. We will sleep in shifts until morning.

Jay returns with his arms full of thick sacks and lays them out next to each other in front of a long, cushioned seat—the couch, as he called it.

His kindness surprises me. I know it is due to whatever power I currently wield over him, but I get the sense that he would have offered us shelter without it. I do not wish to take advantage of this man. It feels wrong.

When his eyes meet mine again, I place my hand over my heart and bow. "Thank you for your generosity. I am called Lukassanai."

His eyes continue to look hazy, but when I envision breaking the bond between us like a sword slicing through the air, I feel the release of his mind as well. He blinks several times and says, "Jay. I-I'm Jay. Did I already say that?"

I offer him a warm grin. "You did."

An hour later, my brothers and I are wrapped in our sleeping bags on the floor of Jay's home, surrounded by the small Starburst wrappers we now know not to eat, and our bellies are full of the delightfully sweet candy. I truly cannot imagine a tastier food than this, which makes it particularly strange that Zevssanai does not seem to enjoy them at all.

"Zevssanai, you *joshik,*" Kyanssanai chides him. When his eyes land on the small pile of uneaten Starburst next to me, he dives toward it, arms outstretched. "You have more of the orange ones. Give them here."

I do happily. The pink ones are by far the best anyway.

"Easy fellas," Jay says as he settles in the cushioned chair next to the couch. "Talia's on her way here with Taco Bell. She always brings food home after her shifts, and this time I told her to bring as much as she could carry." He takes a deep pull from the can in his hand—a liquid called "beer" and gives us a strange look. "Okay, let's talk assimilation. If you don't want it to be obvious to everyone that you just escaped from a cult, some changes need to be made."

"What kind of changes?" Axilssanai asks, lifting a brow.

"Well, your names, for starters. They're very...unique, but you should shorten them."

"Make our names shorter?" Kyanssanai asks, incredulous. "Why is that necessary?"

Jay smirks. "Because people, particularly White people, can't handle long or unique names. No offense."

There is no offense felt, of course, because white is not our true shade.

"My last name is Hoàng, and even though it's one syllable, most people mess it up when they try to say it," he explains. "So maybe you guys should just take the first syllable or two in your names and go by that." He points at me, "You'd be Luka," then he points at Axilssanai, "Axil," and he goes down the line, "Mylo, Zev, and Kyan."

I find that I do not dislike the sound of these shorter names, and if it will make us seem more human, then we should certainly take his advice. Looking at my brothers, who are all nodding or smiling, it is clear they agree.

"Now, what are your last names?" Jay asks.

"Last names?" Mylo asks with an exaggerated gulp. We did not consider this part.

Jay nods. "Yeah."

We all have very long names. My given name is Lukassanai Finai iy Xen Dwai, but which of those additional names should I use as a last name? Or would it be better to use something else entirely?

The five of us exchange nervous glances until finally Zev says, "We do not have last names."

Axil quickly adds, "Or if we did, the cult leaders did not tell us what they are."

"My gods, who is that?" Mylo asks, pointing to a large rectangular photograph of a beautiful woman in a white dress standing above a steel grate of some kind. The bottom half of her dress swirls up around her hips. Mylo is practically drooling at the sight of it. Admittedly, it is difficult to look away from.

"That's Marilyn Monroe," Jay says with a laugh. "Shit, man. You guys really have been living under a rock."

More like on a rock, far, far away, but there is no need to correct our new friend.

"Monroe," Axil mutters under his breath. "That is a pleasing name."

"*Kov*," I say, nodding in agreement. That will do just fine as our last name.

A moment later, the front door swings open and a small female with light brown skin, thick, curved eyebrows and a large knot atop her head enters smelling of meat and hot oil while carrying two large bags in her tiny arms. "Food's here!"

"Yesss," Jay hisses in triumph as he gets to his feet and grabs the bags from her hands. "Guys, this is my girlfriend, Talia. Talia, my ne—"

"Your latest strays," she interrupts, then turns to Jay. "Babe, when are you going to learn that you can't just let anyone in off the street?" Then she turns to face us once more. "They look like hot janitors."

He stops pulling the bell tacos, or whatever he called them, from the bags and gives her a serious look. "These white boys had never heard of the Dave Matthews Band or Starburst. What'd you expect me to do? Just leave them out there on their own?"

"Oof, Jesus," she says, shaking her head. "That does sound dire." Talia steps in front of us and crosses her arms across her chest. Then she paces in front of us as she sizes us up, one by one. "Fine, they can stay, but I get to be in charge of the makeovers."

Jay throws his head back and laughs wildly. "Deal."

"Um," Zev asks in a quiet, nervous tone, "what is a makeover?"

Talia smiles wickedly. "You'll see."

# CHAPTER 3

## LUKA

"*I* have grown quite tired of this, Talia," Kyan says with a groan as he turns in a circle for her. She sits on a blue velvet stool in the middle of the male changing area. Mirrors cover the walls and the doors to our changing rooms. "How many more shirts must I try on?"

She gives him a thumbs up on his current shirt and pants, a gesture we have learned on this outing means she approves. Kyan lets out a relieved sigh as he heads back into his room.

"I concur," I add, smoothing the front of the third long-sleeved Henley shirt Talia has selected for me, just in a slightly different shade of gray than the previous two. Makeovers are a taxing ordeal. She made it seem like a thrilling adventure, but my brothers and I have spent hours taking off shirts and pants only to put more on and model them for her. There is nothing thrilling about it.

"Luka, push up the sleeves just a bit," she instructs. "Show off those forearms. Those are your moneymakers."

I do as she says despite her strange wording, and I am rewarded with an enthusiastic thumbs up and bright smile. "Okay, fine. We can be done," she says, getting to her feet and flipping through the piles of clothes she selected for each of us. "I think this is a good start. Just over a week's worth of outfits for each of you, plus a few sets of pajamas."

"May I wear this out of the store?" Mylo asks, his hands running down his stomach, over the soft fabric of his red-and-blue-striped sweater vest. "It is delightfully soft."

"Of course," she tells him. "In fact, you all need to pick an outfit to wear back to Jay's." She holds out a wrinkled brown paper bag. "Let's just toss the stuff you borrowed from him in here."

As exhausting as this was, I am glad to have some attire that actually fits my body. Talia did not allow us to wear our silver jumpsuits here, leaving us no other choice but to change into the largest items of clothing Jay could find in his closet, which were not many. The only pants of his that would fit over our thighs were what he called "sweatpants," and those were extremely tight.

The first pair Axil donned tore at the seams when he attempted to pull them over his hips, and the second pair did not even cover his ankles.

When Jay saw the pair I put on, his gaze drifted to my cock and he muttered something under his breath about a garter snake versus an anaconda, which I did not understand. Perhaps it was a common human joke of some kind?

Talia rips the tags from the items we decide to wear out of the massive department store, and we each carry our pile of new clothes out of the dressing room and toward the front of the store.

"Jesus, it's packed in here today," Talia mumbles as a young woman darts in front of us with her screeching child in her arms.

Talia guides us to the back of a line filled with people waiting to drop their items on a moving black table, ultimately leading to a very bored looking boy who carelessly stuffs the items in a plastic bag.

There are so many sights, sounds, and smells here that my eyes begin to water. Why do these people willingly cram themselves into such crowded spaces? Earth is a strange place.

We are second in line when Talia turns to us and says, "Okay, do you guys want to pay for your stuff separately or all together?"

Mylo tilts his head and lifts an eyebrow. "Pay? I do not understand."

"We need to pay for these clothes," she replies. "How much money do you have on you?"

"We have no money," Axil says.

Talia's eyes widen and she lets out a whispered curse. "I can't believe I didn't ask you before we left. Of course you don't have money. You escaped that cult with only your weird space suits." She picks through the pile of clothes on the moving table, looking at the numbers on the tags. "We need to put this stuff back."

Mylo begins gathering the clothing in his arms when the bored boy behind the moving table says, "Find everything you were looking for today?" as he reaches for the clothes left on the table and pulls them toward the beeping machine in front of him.

"Uh, actually, we need to put a few of these ba–" Talia begins.

"Some of us are in a hurry here," the lanky man behind us hollers at us.

"Sorry," Talia says, her cheeks turning red. She urges Mylo to drop the clothes back on the table. "I can, um…" Her gaze shifts to the bored boy. "Can I split this purchase between a few credit cards?"

Zev seems to sense Talia's distress and holds his hand above her open wallet. "You do not need to acquire clothing for us, Talia. All will be well. We shall find another way."

She smiles up at him warmly and shakes her head. "I can't let you guys walk around Boston in those cult outfits. Really, it's fine." She clears her throat and starts moving the clothes into smaller piles. "Just promise you'll pay me back someday, okay?"

My stomach twists at the sight of Talia scrambling to find payment for our new clothing. It is clear she does not have adequate funds for this purchase, and even though we do not yet know the total amount, I get the impression it is beyond what she is used to spending.

That she is willing to provide us with new clothing at all speaks to her gracious spirit. She and Jay have been kind to us. I must fix this.

If we were still on Sufoi, this would not be an issue. There, when an item of clothing was in need of repair or replacement, we would submit a request and the issue would be resolved that very day. Due to the extreme physical demands of being the king's assassins, our clothing was provided without charge. But those titles mean nothing here.

"I don't think you can buy clothes with food stamps, okay, honey?" The man behind us shouts with a low chuckle.

"I'm not trying to do that," Talia replies in a soft, shaky voice. Leaning closer to the bored boy, she asks, "Is there any way you can put a few of these on hold? I can come back tomorrow when you open and pay for them then."

I do not catch all the words that fall from the man's lips, but the first two are, "Lazy fucking." The third word is the one that causes Talia's eyes to fill with tears.

"Never mind," she mutters to the bored boy. "I'll just get them all now." She wipes the tears from her cheeks and hands him three small cards. "If you can split it up evenly between these, I'd appreciate it."

The boy does nothing to calm Talia. He nods and takes her cards as she requested. And the man behind us is still grumbling about how long we are taking. It is then that I decide to test my abilities, as I have grown tired of this man and his unkind judgments of the woman who has been incredibly generous to us. I refuse to allow him to continue exhibiting such disgusting behavior without any repercussions.

I turn to face him, and he swallows as he takes me in. He is shorter than I am, but not by much. His frame is long and lean, his dark hair is unkempt in a way that does not seem intentional, and his clothes are stained and rumpled. It is clear this man dislikes himself as much as he clearly dislikes those around him, but that is not reason enough for me to offer him empathy. This man embarrassed Talia and made her cry, and for that, he must suffer.

Staring into his light brown eyes, I watch as the muscles around his mouth relax, and his heartbeat gets louder in my ears. I have him trapped. As his breathing slows, I get a sense of his mind, and wow, his brain is mushier than Jay's. I wonder what I could make this man do before he snapped out of my trance? Could I make him lay on the floor in this middle of this establishment and beg for his mother as urine soaks his pants? Could I have him strip down to nothing and cover his body with Starburst wrappers? Such tempting ideas to humiliate him, but no, I must not give in. We have a problem, and he holds the solution in his weak hands.

I gesture for him to lean toward me, which he does, instantly. I whisper my demands as he nods his head. Then he gently nudges me and my brothers aside and offers his card to the bored boy. "My apologies, ma'am. I'd like to atone for my horrible comments by paying for your items."

Talia jerks back in surprise. The bored boy does as well, and his face transforms with the sudden rush of emotion. "Seriously?" he asks.

"Yes," the man says as he looks at Talia. "It's the least I can do."

I pat the man on the back and smile at Talia. "It is certainly the least he can do."

Talia eyes me suspiciously but does not hesitate to let the man pay. "Okay, well…" she begins, as the bored boy slides the card through the machine. "Thanks."

Talia puts her cards away as the boy shoves our new clothes into several plastic bags.

I suppose I could let the man out of the trance now that the transaction is complete, but I decide to wait. We are not done with him just yet.

Talia leans against me as we walk toward the exit. "What the fuck was that? How did you convince him to pay?"

"I reasoned with him," I say with a shrug, letting a playful smirk linger on my lips. There is no easy way to explain what I did, and despite Talia's kindness, I do not trust her with our true identities, which includes what we are capable of.

This is also a new ability for me, and even if I did trust Talia with our secrets, I am not ready to divulge this skill until I understand the extent of it.

Talia shakes her head in awe. "You know what? Fuck it. I don't even care what you did. I'm just glad you did it."

"Wait," I tell her and my brothers as we step outside the store.

Kyan looks around us as if he is ready to go into battle. "What are we waiting for?"

I smile. "Our new friend has a gift for us."

The man steps outside a moment later, and his eyes brighten with recognition when he spots me. "Ah, there you are." He strides toward us and holds out his hand. Several folded green papers rest in his palm. "Here's the rest I owe you. Have a great day."

I take the papers and hand them to Talia, then I look back at the man and do the same as I did with Jay; I envision a sword slicing through the air between us, and I feel the mushiness of his mind slip from my grasp. Once freed from the trance, the man's eyes narrow on us, and I see the resentment return. To keep him from suspecting anything, I say, "Thank you for sharing that with us, friend. A bright future awaits you."

He looks confused and irritated, but confusion is the dominant emotion, and that has him wandering away from us without saying another word.

"Luka, this is way more than I put on my card," Talia says. "There's like, five hundred dollars here. I can't take this. You guys have nothing. You should have it."

I put up a hand, refusing her offer. "You shall keep it. I am quite certain we will be fine."

She chuckles. "Somehow, I am too."

Hours after we arrive back at Jay's and show him our new attire, he encourages us to "rock our baller outfits" at the nearby dance hall. Both he and Talia have to work, so we agree to go alone. I am reluctant to interact with humans without him close by, in case we need assistance with translating human slang, but this will also be an opportunity for us to practice blending in with people.

Not long after we arrive, we discover a group of males who call themselves "hedge fund managers." Mylo introduces himself, and they invite us to join them at their table. These men throw their cash papers all over their tiny, white-powder-covered table, they are incredibly cruel to the workers who serve them, and they seem to treat the females who enter the dance hall as if they are as disposable as the napkins that come with their expensive beverages.

For some reason, however, they enjoy our company. I am inclined to believe this is due to the positive attention we are receiving from the women in attendance. They like looking at us. Clearly, the skin shade we chose for our masks makes us appealing. I suppose it is a good thing, and by the wide smiles on my brothers' faces, I can tell they are enjoying the attention. The burn in my chest keeps me from feeling the same. The only eyes I want running along my body are my mate's. I just wish I knew how to find her. Her scent is nowhere to be found in this dance hall, and the absence of it serves as a reminder of how close I came to locating her and making her mine.

Axil peels himself away from a thin woman with blonde hair and long legs and nudges my arm. "What are you waiting for, brother?"

I wait for him to explain further, but he does not. "Hm?"

"Look at all of this," he says, gesturing to the money strewn about on the table. "Let us collect our bounty and go back to Jay's." He lets out a loud yawn. "I want to slumber soon. Use your magic."

It appears I must act fact, because if Axil gets too tired, he will become unbearably cranky, and I do not wish to unleash that side of him onto the public.

It turns out that hedge fund managers have a seemingly endless supply of money. Their brains are the softest I have encountered thus far, likely due to the various substances they inhale through their nostrils, and they are the most gratifying to take from, given their atrocious behavior and terrible decisions. By the end of the evening, Mylo has acquired a new watch that is apparently quite expensive, given that the man who gave it to him kept saying it was a "brand-new Rolex," and we have accrued five thousand dollars in cash.

I have a feeling this is going to be a very lucrative endeavor.

# CHAPTER 4

## HARPER

*TWO WEEKS LATER...*

"This is it—a new beginning. A new me," I tell myself as I look in the bathroom mirror and fuss with my new, chin-length blonde hair. Despite the dozen or so little hairs that seem determined to stand up straight along my part no matter how much hairspray I apply, I'm going to leave this house with a positive attitude. I've never been this happy on a Monday morning, and this particular Monday is different. I'm officially divorced, and my formerly long dark-brown hair is now extremely short and a popping shade of platinum.

*Freddy would've hated this haircut,* I can't help but think with a smirk. He threw a tantrum every time I mentioned even getting a trim. In his eyes, my hair could never be long enough. He liked it full and long with big curls, but when I wore it like that, I was constantly blowing hair off my face and counting down the seconds until I could throw it up in a bun without him groaning in disappointment.

Our marriage wasn't always bad. For years, we were inseparable.

He was my best friend. Then our life changed when I had my accident, and when I look back at the many peaks and valleys of our relationship, I know that was the moment we started growing apart.

He was supportive during my recovery and was never a dick about my new physical limitations, but ultimately, he didn't want his life to change, and mine already had. So much of what we had in common were physical activities. We'd play tennis and softball, we'd go hiking in the summer and skiing as often as possible in the winter. But when your wife crashes into a tree on her skis and becomes permanently disabled, you need to accept the fact that the time you spend together is going to be different. That's not something he could handle.

He chose to continue doing all that stuff, just without me by his side. I understood. Or, I tried to, at least. My accident wasn't his fault, and he shouldn't be punished for what happened. I didn't want to be the reason he lost so many things that he loved. I guess I just thought he loved me more, and that he'd choose me over the stuff I could no longer do. He didn't, and that crushed me. I wanted to yell at him, beg him to love me more and spend time with me, but every time I came close to getting the words out, I swallowed them instead. Why should I have to beg my husband to love me? Then, one day I woke up and realized I was sharing my life with someone I no longer knew.

That's all in the past though.

Big changes are happening, and I'm ready to get back out into the world again.

The moment I step outside, a blast of bitter cold whacks me in the face, but even that won't get me down, not when I look this cute. Putting in my earbuds, I scroll through my iPod until I find Fergie's "Glamorous" and crank it up.

I'm almost inclined to skip as I walk down the street to work, but since I physically can't skip, I sing instead.

*"Ooh, the flossy f*-uuucking hell!" I scream as I trip over a crack in the sidewalk and go flying forward.

Luckily, I'm able to shift my body enough that I land on my good side, protecting my left hip and knee from smashing into the concrete.

My cane is a few feet away, and I groan as I roll onto my stomach and crawl over to it. I get up slowly, wiping dirt and unidentified muck from my jacket, but I let out a relieved sigh when I find my iPod still safely tucked in my pocket.

"Gonna take a lot more than that, bitch," I say, looking up at the sky. I'm not necessarily talking to God. In fact, I don't know who I'm talking to, but it had to be said. I'm not about to let a little fall rattle me.

When I arrive at the vet clinic ten minutes later, I'm greeted at the back door with a dramatic gasp from my favorite technician, Ryan. "Shit, doc! I didn't even recognize you," he says. "Love the hair."

Eliza, our main receptionist, bursts through the back entrance right behind me and shrieks at the top of her lungs. "Oh my god!" Then she throws her bag down on the floor and plucks at the ends of my hair. "It's wicked short. And blonde. Major Gwen Stefani vibes. I'm dying right now. It looks so hot."

Blood rushes to my cheeks at all the attention.

"What made you do it?" Eliza asks, referring to my new, very different look. "Is this because you're officially single now?"

I forgot that I texted her about that on Friday afternoon, thirty minutes after my lawyer called to say my divorce was finalized and twenty minutes after I emptied my third bottle of Shipyard pumpkin ale.

"It's not about that. I just wanted a change," I tell her and Ryan. I'm not trying to look good for anyone else but me. After being dragged through emotional hell with the divorce proceedings, and the fact that Freddy got to keep our beautiful Beacon Hill house while I got stuck with a cramped one-bedroom townhouse in Mission Hill, I needed a drastic change.

"Well, that's it," Eliza says, taking a sip of her Dunkin' Donuts iced coffee and slamming it on the edge of the x-ray table. "We're going out tonight. I know the bouncer at The Shadow Den. He can get us in. No cover."

Ryan leans his chin on the top of the mop handle in his hands. "For real? I've been dying to check that place out."

A scowl starts to form on my face. "A club? On a Monday night?"

Ryan gently elbows my side. "Come on, doc. Have a drink with us."

Eliza puts her hands on her hips and huffs. "You've gotta get back out there, and you wouldn't have done this," she gestures at my hair, "if a little part of you didn't want to mingle with some singles."

"So you want me to go out on a Monday night, to a club—the kind of place I hate—after bailing on me for the Trippin' Billygoats show?" I ask Eliza in an accusing tone.

"Ugh, I'm sorry," Eliza replies with a dramatic slap of her palm against her forehead. "I owe you several iced coffees for that. How was it, by the way?"

"It was amazing. I screamed the lyrics to *Two Step* so loud, I lost my voice. But I gave my brother your ticket, and he was wicked high on mushrooms the whole night, so he ended up having a deep conversation with a barstool until the show ended."

Ryan chuckles. "Sounds about right."

Eliza plasters on her sad puppy face until I cave.

"Fine…what time?" I ask, defeated. Eliza and Ryan are in their mid-twenties. Babies. Beautiful, exuberant babies who can drink and party until three in the morning and still get up at seven for work. I'm in my thirties and haven't been to a club in…I don't know, years?

"We usually meet up at ten," Eliza says, but when she sees my eyes widen in horror, she adds, "but let's call it nine, and if you're not having the best time ever, you can leave at ten."

A guaranteed out? I love that. "Okay, deal," I say with a sigh. "But I'm getting us bottle service so we have a place to sit." I hear Ryan and Eliza cheering quietly behind me as I walk toward my office. They probably knew I would do that, because whenever the three of us hang out, I pay for extras like that to ensure my comfort, since I can only be on my feet for so long without my cane.

It doesn't bother me though because they deserve it, and every once in a while, I can afford to give them that kind of treat. They work hard and always have my back when Dr. Brooks and I get into a tiff, which is fairly often.

Speak of the devil.

"Ah, Harper. Good morning," Dr. Brooks says without looking away from his computer when I enter the little office we share.

"Morning, Dr. Brooks," I reply, my teeth grinding at his passive-aggressive refusal to call me Dr. O'Connor. It's one of many things I dislike about this man, along with the fact that he speaks to me like I'm still a vet school student and not a skilled doctor. I've been working here for eight years. My vet school days are far behind me.

It's not as if he does this to the male vets we meet at conferences though. They could be mere days past graduation, and he'd still address them as "Dr. Whomever." Yet I'm just Harper. It makes me want to sprinkle shards of glass in his tuna salad.

Plus, he refuses to make me a managing partner at this veterinary practice, despite the many referral programs I've set up with local rescue groups, the newer and more effective preventative supplements I convinced him to get for our patients, and the sheer number of clients I've brought in just by networking with the staffers at surrounding emergency clinics.

Dr. Brooks has owned this practice for over a decade, sees just three patients a day, then leaves by lunch to play golf. I'm usually here at least ten hours a day, my clients love me, and my patients love me—even the cranky ones who growl or hiss at everyone else. I deserve a stake in the business I've worked so hard to help build.

Maybe then my parents would stop showering my brother with praise just because he has an MD after his name. He's a mediocre doctor, not terrible, but not that great either. And still, they're definitely prouder of him than they are of me. He was always the golden child, even when we were little, and I have no idea why. He's half-assed everything he's ever done, and my parents treat him as if he's on the verge of curing cancer, which is about as likely to happen as me skiing again.

"We really need to start pushing the laser therapy treatments," he says, still staring at the computer. "That machine isn't going to pay for itself."

This is a conversation we've had every week since he got that machine a few months ago. The therapy laser was free with the purchase of the surgical laser, and he took out a hefty loan for the latter. We use the surgical laser every day, but the therapy laser, as far as I can tell, doesn't provide as much relief to patients with chronic pain as was promised by the sales rep who sold them to us, which is why I haven't recommended it.

"I just wish we had more data on the positive results because the few patients who have tried it aren't seeing much of a difference, and I'm reluctant to keep pushing a treatment that doesn't work," I explain.

He finally turns in his chair and his eyes bug out at the sight of my hair. "Wow, you, uh, changed your hair."

"I did," I reply with a smile as I run my fingers through it.

He nods, his mouth still hanging open. "It's very…extreme."

*Extreme.* That's the word he chooses.

"Well, anyway," he says with a cough, "it's not like the treatment hurts the patient, and good medicine is all about the upsell, you know?"

Wrong. That's inherently incorrect.

"It's about the extra treatments we can provide to our patients that will improve their lives," he continues. "And, at worst, this treatment does nothing, but at best, it provides immense relief to dogs and cats with arthritis. We won't be able to collect the data you want without testing it on our own patients."

"Actually, at worst, this treatment does nothing and the client wastes money they already can't afford to spend," I tell him. "That weakens the trust they have in us, which will prevent them from agreeing to future treatments their pet actually needs to survive. Or they take their business elsewhere and we never see them again."

Dr. Brooks rolls his eyes right on cue. It's not the first time I've voiced my concerns, and it won't be the last. "Just do it," he mutters. He begins to turn back to his computer, but then stops. "This is an example of why I'm hesitant to make you a managing partner, Harper. I need someone with more of a business mindset."

Before I can offer the sort of biting, unprofessional retort that Dr.

Brooks deserves to hear, Eliza pokes her head in. "Dr. Brooks, your first patient is in room one. Loofah the cat with a cut on his paw."

Dr. Brooks clears his throat, straightens his tie, and refuses to meet my gaze as he heads toward the exam room.

"Oh, wait," I whisper before he opens the door. "Loofah's owner just separated from her husband and had to move back in with her parents, so her finances are tight right now. You might want to kee—"

Dr. Brooks waves his hand dismissively before I can finish. "I don't need her life story." Then he goes into the room with a scowl.

My good mood deflates significantly, and it's all his fault. Prick.

* * *

A remix of Rihanna's "Umbrella" blares through the speakers around us as Ryan, Eliza, and I shake our asses on the dance floor of The Shadow Den. The second the song ends and one I don't recognize begins, I slowly head back to our table. I know my knee will be wicked sore tonight—it is most nights—so I'm only going to dance to songs I absolutely love. Then the pain will at least be worth it.

I sink into the cushions of our booth and swallow an entire bottle of water in three gulps. Still a bit buzzed from two Jack and Cokes, I smile as I watch Ryan and Eliza grind against their respective dance partners.

Eliza's got a shorter, dark-haired bodybuilder-type guy wrapped around her, and Ryan is gripping the hips of a thin man wearing a tie-dye tank top as he thrusts into him from behind. They're so cute, my heart swells. I'm not sure when it happened, but these two feel like younger siblings to me. They're a source of endless entertainment, but I'm also compelled to protect and support them.

Surprised by how packed this place is on a Monday night, my eyes dart around the room, scanning the people dancing or hanging out in their private booths. The moment I lock eyes with a man in the VIP section, my heart stops. Three beautiful women surround him, their arms wrapped around his neck, and they're hanging on his every word. Next to him are seven other guys, four of whom have similar builds and facial features, also draped in hot women. They must be related. And these women aren't just hot, they're Playboy Bunny hot.

So why is *he* still staring at *me?*

My throat goes dry the moment he separates himself from his admirers and walks toward me. He's huge, over seven feet tall, and muscles cover every inch of his massive frame. Tattoos wrap around his forearms and disappear beneath the rolled cuffs of his sleeves. His pale-blue button-down shirt and black pants are definitely on the tighter side, but not so tight that he looks like he might Hulk out of them with a single flex. He must've had those clothes tailored because no one his size could buy clothes off the rack and have them fit that well.

I find myself gawking at the hard line of his jaw, his intense gaze, and the playful smirk that tugs at his soft lips. He's almost too beautiful to look at—an otherworldly beauty that doesn't seem possible for mere mortals. Where the hell did this guy come from? He must be a model, or professional athlete, or something, just in town for a night or two before he flies back to Los Angeles, or Paris, or wherever it is extremely hot people come from.

"Hi," he says as he sits next to me.

When he gives me an expectant look, I realize I've been quiet too long while ogling him, so I nervously mutter, "Oh, hi. Yeah, hi."

"You are a magnificent creature," he says, his voice so low and throaty it has me clenching my thighs. "Your scent is intoxicating. I should very much like to shove my cock inside you and feel your wet heat."

*What?* Of all the words I expected to come out of his mouth, those were not among them.

"Would you like to come to my home so we may fornicate?"

I don't understand what's happening or how I'm supposed to react. I suppose I should find his straightforward approach to picking up women refreshing. He stated his intentions clearly, that's for sure. I would assume that maybe there's a language barrier here, if not for the lack of an accent. He does have a strange way of speaking though. His words are stilted and too formal, which seems extremely odd for someone his age.

When I look at the booth he came from, I notice the women who were hanging all over him are now pointing at me and whispering to each other, and the guys who he must be related to glare in our direction. It makes my skin crawl with anxiety, reminding me of the moments I was bullied in high school for having thick thighs and a soft belly. Is this some kind of prank? Pretend to hit on the fat, disabled girl for a couple of cheap laughs? Hell-the-fuck-no. I'm not letting this douchebag belittle me.

"You know what? I'll pass," I say in a biting tone. "Seems like you have plenty of potential fornication partners back where you came from, so run along now."

He jerks back, looking startled and confused. The gall this guy has. Did he really think I'd spread my legs just because he gave me a moment of—incredibly awkward—attention?

"What part of that did you not understand?" I ask, shooing him away with my hand. "Go on. Get out of here."

"I am deeply sorry," he says in a genuine tone that catches me off guard. He puts his hand over his heart and adds, "I have said the wrong thing. I am called Luka. May I buy you a beverage to make up for it?"

I gesture toward the bottles of liquor and several mixers that remain at our table. "No, I'm good. Thanks."

Luka leans in, staring intently into my eyes as if he's trying to see into my soul. "You enjoy talking to me. You find me pleasant to look at, and you want me to press my lips against yours." Then he holds himself perfectly still, as if we've entered a staring contest I didn't consent to.

I have no idea what kind of game he's playing, but it's time to put an end to it. Leaning forward and holding his gaze, I say, "Sorry, Luka, but no the fuck I do not."

His face scrunches up in disbelief. "No? To which part?"

I pour myself another Jack and Coke and lean back in my seat, refusing to meet his gaze. "No to all the parts."

Luka's nostrils flare at my words, and a low growl rumbles from his chest. Then he shouts, "Fine then!" and leaves.

"Damn, who was that tasty tree of a man?" Eliza asks when she and Ryan come back to the table.

I'm reluctantly admiring Luka's firm ass as he strides back to his booth. "Just some weird, entitled shithead I'll never see again."

# CHAPTER 5

## LUKA

"*T*his is a catastrophe!" I shout as I stomp down the sidewalk and into the cold night, my brothers running to keep up with me. "I do not know what to do."

My draxilio growls at my lack of action. *Go back inside. Claim her.*

*I cannot,* I send back. *My influence did not work on her. She shunned me.*

Axil is the first one to reach my side. "Stop, brother. Tell us what has happened. Who was she?"

"My mate," I begin, my chest heaving with fury and disappointment, "does not want me. She was not enchanted by my offer of sex, and she did not react at all when I tried to use my powers to convince her otherwise."

"She could not be influenced?" Zev asks, tilting his head to the side. "That is odd. Is she the first human you have failed to influence with your powers?"

"*Kov!*" I shout. "I do not know how to win her heart." I start pacing in a small circle as I determine my next move. "Humans are different. They cannot scent their mate. They do not experience the mate signals that we do. They lack any kind of awareness when the creature they are meant to spend eternity with is right in front of them."

"Perhaps you did it incorrectly," Kyan suggests. "This is a new power for you, and you have only been using it for two weeks now."

"I did not do it incorrectly," I reply with a sneer. "There was nothing coming from her. I could not feel her pulse, determine the pace of her breathing, or sense the malleability of her brain."

Mylo sighs as he scratches his chin. "Is this the first female you have used your powers on? From what I have seen, there have only been males."

Mylo's observation is correct. Upon discovering my ability to influence the minds of humans, I have used it many times, mostly to steal their money or valuables. It takes less than a minute for me to get a human male under my spell and convince him that he is eager to hand over whatever cash he may have in his wallet or the expensive watch on his wrist.

But wait, males are not the only ones I have used my power on. "There was the older female who entered Jay's pawn shop and told him to return to his country. Remember?"

Mylo smiles at the memory. I did not use my power to take her money, however. I merely convinced her that her life would be incomplete if she did not purchase a damaged musical instrument in Jay's shop that he called a "tuba" for three hundred dollars more than was listed on the tag.

"Ah, *kov*," Mylo says. "And you found her brain quite mushy?"

"Extremely mushy," I reply. "I could feel her. I did not feel my mate at all."

"Do not forget about the female at the department of motor vehicles. We would not have our human documents without the use of your power on her that day," Zev notes, giving me an encouraging smile.

Then an extremely frustrating realization enters my head. "I did not even learn my mate's name. How will I find her again?" I must solve this immediately. She does not have to pledge her devotion to me now, but I need a name in order to begin wooing her properly. Before I can shove past my brothers and head back toward the dance hall, Axil steps in front of me, blocking my path.

"No." He sees the anger in my eyes and adds, "It is not the time. She made her feelings clear. You must leave her be. You will find her again. I know it."

He is right. I would rather fly into Earth's fiery sun than admit it, but he is right. I must let her go—not forever—but for tonight.

Kyan clears his throat. "Or you could forget about her entirely. She rejected you, Luka. Humans are weak and irritating anyway."

I should consider Kyan's comment from a place of sensitivity. He was born angry, and the unkind treatment we received from our handlers made it worse. He is the only one who did not wish to participate in this mission to Earth and remains convinced that his fated mate does not exist, and even if he or she did, they would not be worth the time and energy required to make them happy.

Instead, I match Kyan's pessimism with barely controlled rage as I step into his space and stand nose to nose with him. "Dip your snout, *crana*," I growl through gritted teeth. It is not a phrase I casually toss about as it was weaponized against us on Sufoi. My brothers know this, so when I do say it, it is a clear warning that I am on the edge of melting the skin off their faces and they need to know their place.

He says nothing, just lets his shoulders sag as he reluctantly lowers his head.

Axil and Zev each put a hand on my shoulders to calm me as they turn me around and walk in the direction of our new home. It takes but a handful of minutes for us to arrive. A block from Jay's apartment, we discovered vacancies in both apartments on the top floor of this newly constructed building. After knocking down the walls that kept our dwellings separate and using my powers to convince the building manager that he had previously approved the changes we made, we filled it with items human dwellings have and made it an acceptable shelter.

We kick off our boots by the front door, unmask our skin and horns, and settle on our pale-green velvet sectional in the living room. It is nice to have a space wherein we can exist as our true selves. "Axil, send a digital note to Jay and ask if he is available to come see us. I would like his advice on this situation with my mate."

Axil lets out a pleased grunt a moment later. "Five minutes." We return to our pale human masks the moment the buzzer sounds from our front door.

Jay and Talia carry a tray of homemade brownies as they enter, along with several cardboard boxes containing "pee-zah" and with a single bite of the cheese-covered triangular dough, my mood has improved almost completely.

"Here is your cut for the day," Axil says to Jay as he hands him a thick wad of cash. Jay and Talia are aware that we have been able to separate the hedge fund managers from their money through nefarious methods, but they do not know specifics. In fact, Talia was insistent upon us not sharing the truth of our power—she does not wish to be implicated if we were ever to get caught—and I was more than pleased to keep that secret.

Because they have been, and continue to be, so kind to me and my brothers, giving us shelter the first night we arrived and giving us lessons on how to interact with humans, they deserve a portion of our earnings.

"So, tell us what happened," Talia says through a mouthful of crust as she sits on the arm of the couch.

I relay the exchange between my mate and me, and before I am even finished speaking, Talia yells, "Oh dear god, you did not." She throws her half-eaten slice back into the box and claps her hands. "Okay, first of all, what the fuck? Second of all, the word fornicate is not and never will be sexy. Third of all, seriously, what the fuck?"

Jay holds his face in his hands. "Dude, I know you guys haven't had it easy since you busted outta that cult, but we really gotta work on your vocabulary and overall ability to socialize with other people. Your game is mad weak."

"Yup. Yup, yup, yup," Talia says with an exaggerated nod. "Let's just steer clear of mentioning your cock in the first few minutes of meeting a woman, K? Maybe avoid commenting on her scent too? 'Cuz that's kinda strange when you don't have an established connection with her, even if you're complimenting the way she smells. Offer to buy her a drink before you say anything else because that's a common icebreaker for people at a bar, and I have a feeling she would've said yes if you led with that. And I know I said this already, but I feel like it's really important you hear it again—drop the word *fornicate*."

"I have said all those things to the many females I have fornicated with over the last two weeks, and they were not bothered in the least," I point out.

"Yeah, but you also didn't care what they thought of you, right? It was just sex," Talia adds.

I nod. What she says is true. I have put very little effort into impressing the women I have met thus far. Often, I do not even need to ask if they would like to fornicate. I tell them my name and that I am pleased by their appearance, and suddenly they are unbuttoning my shirt and pulling me into the dance hall bathroom as their lips smack along the length of my throat. This is all without the use of my power. I did not use it on the females I have bedded because I did not need to. If any of them had rejected my advances, I would have simply moved on to another. But that has not occurred. My mate was the first woman to reject me.

Jay holds a hand up. "I'd also like to add that the five of you can't share a single phone. You each need your own."

"But why?" Zev replies earnestly. "We are always together. We do not need more than one phone."

Talia and Jay exchange a look I cannot decipher. "Yeah, but that's going to change." His gaze lands on me. "Luka, are really you gonna bring your brothers along on dates if you end up getting this girl to like you? You'll lead your own lives eventually, might as well start now."

I had not considered this. I knew I would spend time with my mate alone once I found her, but I assumed my brothers and I would remain in the same dwelling once I was mated, as all families do on Sufoi. They need me. They have always needed me to watch over them. Our handlers only served to remind us of everything we could not be or have because we were genetically altered and not pure draxilios. They did not fill any sort of parental role. That responsibility was mine.

In the handful of times my brothers were on their own on Sufoi, they got into trouble. Lots of it. I cannot allow that to happen here. It would surely lead to the authorities learning what we are. But does that mean I must choose between my mate and my brothers? That is a choice I cannot make.

* * *

Several days pass, one blending into the next. I have existed in a never-ending cycle of roaming around the city alone during the day, looking for my mate, and stealing from finance bros at dance halls at night. My brothers remain at home during the day, as per my orders, watching TV and bickering over who maintains possession of the remote.

Even now, I am wandering aimlessly through the neighborhood.

Suddenly, the wind shifts, and her scent reaches my nose.

Wet, heavy snow falls from the sky, but the moment I detect her presence, I am wrapped in a euphoric warmth that could only occur from the nearness of one's mate. I follow the scent until I see a human on the other side of the street, walking in the opposite direction. There is no one else in the vicinity, so it must be her.

She wears a long black coat with a hood that obscures her face from my view, but a flash of her yellow hair confirms that she is who I have been looking for. She walks with a cane, and there is a stiffness in the way the left side of her body moves as she walks. I am desperate to spend my days massaging her body until every ounce of pain evaporates.

She enters a facility with the words "Veterinary Clinic" on the front of the building, and instinctively, I follow. Once inside, I am greeted by a tiny woman with long, curly brown hair tucked away in a tight braid, tanned skin, and a probing, fascinated gaze. "Hello, there," she says with a grin. "Do you have an appointment?" Her dark-blue eyes drift down to my empty arms. "Or a pet you'd like the doctor to examine?"

"A...pet? No, I do not," I admit. "But I would like to speak with the woman who just came in here. Is this where she is employed?"

"Short blonde hair?" she asks. When I nod, she looks at her computer screen and says, "Yes, that's Dr. Harper O'Connor. She's in with a patient right now, but I can fit you in as her next appointment. Should be about fifteen minutes." She gets to her feet and greets me at the half-door that separates the lobby from the hallway. "You're going to be in this room here on the right." She gestures to the only open door, and I take a seat on the leather-cushioned bench once inside the room.

My heart feels like it could burst from my chest at this news. "Yes. Fine, that is good. I shall wait," I reply with a wide grin I cannot contain, practically bouncing in place.

I spend the time going over the many normal, human-like things Talia and Jay told me I should say the next time I saw my mate. Most of the phrases seem silly to repeat. Why must I comment on the condition of the weather? We can both see what is happening outside. It seems pointless to discuss, especially since I care nothing about the weather. I want to learn about Harper O'Connor and everything she is willing to share with me, but if that will make me seem less threatening to my mate, then I shall ready myself to describe the wet snow to her in great detail.

The dampened state of my palms frustrates me. Draxilios have such an easier time solidifying their mate bonds. There is none of this courting nonsense. The gods show us who our fated mate is through one or more clear mate signals, and we listen. However, if I were still on Sufoi, I would be alone, mateless, and unworthy of companionship, as our handlers often reminded us. My brothers would be at my side, but I would be alone.

I hear the door to the next room open and the sound of male laughter echoing through the hall. "Well, I guess I'll have to convince you over dinner. What do you say? Pine and Sage at seven?"

"Tonight?" a female voice responds, the word coming out as barely more than a squeak. That is the squeak of my mate, and the sound makes my skin come alive with awareness. Her scent wafts into the room through the crack beneath the door, and my cock hardens once the aroma is deep within my lungs, like a piece of sweet, juicy fruit that I am desperate to taste. "Oh, um…" she trails off. She does not wish to have dinner with this male. I do not need to see her face to sense her reluctance.

The male's feet shuffle, and I hear him say, "Oh come on, you'll love it."

She chuckles nervously.

"Who doesn't love a free dinner? Am I right?" he adds.

I hear the woman who greeted me at the large desk say, "I, personally, love a free dinner."

"See?" he says in a cocky tone. "It'd be pretty rude of you to say no."

The draxilio within me bristles with annoyance. I do not like the way this male speaks to her. The way he pushes her to bend to his will. How well does he even know my mate? Would she actually enjoy the restaurant he has invited her to?

There is also something in the tone of his voice that sets me on edge. Something ugly, sinister. I do not trust him.

My mate remains quiet for a moment longer, then finally says, "Okay, yeah. That sounds nice. I'll see you there at seven."

No. She has agreed to share a meal with this pompous *joshik*? I must convince her to stay far away from him.

The door to the room I am in swings open, and my breath leaves my body entirely when I am greeted with my mate's warm smile. But that smile soon fades when she takes me in.

"You," she mutters quietly, then thumps her cane on the floor, causing her ample breasts to jiggle slightly and making my mouth water. "Aren't you the…the guy from the club? The fornication guy?"

I dip my chin, offering what I hope is a humble half-smile. "I am. My name is Luka. It is an honor to meet you properly, Dr. O'Connor."

"Harper," she whispers, her gaze lingering on my lips. She looks down at my feet, then around the room. "Do you not have a pet with you? What are you doing here?" She steps out into the hall. "Eliza, what's going on exactly?"

The female called Eliza skips down the hall with a mischievous grin. "Look at you, doc! Getting all the gentleman callers today."

Harper does not reply, and her scowl deepens as she stares at Eliza.

Eliza rolls her eyes. "Okay, fine. He didn't have an appointment, or a pet, but he wanted to see you, and, by the way," she points at me as she leans closer to Harper and lowers her voice, "what part of him are you not looking at?"

Harper holds up a hand. "All right, that's enough."

"You can't expect me to look at that jawline and function normally," Eliza replies, shrugging. Then she turns and walks back to her big desk. "That's just unreasonable."

Harper sighs as she turns back to face me. "Look, Luka, I'm not sure why you came down here, but if you don't have a pet, I can't help you."

I stand, reveling in the way Harper's pupils dilate and her throat works as she takes in my full height. She is so tiny standing next to me. I tower over her by almost two feet, and where my body is made of hard lines and thick muscle, she is short and soft all over. My body was built to protect her, and hers was made for me to squeeze, to caress, to worship.

She swallows audibly as her gaze drifts down my chest. There is no fear scent coming off her, so this must mean she is pleased by my form. While I cannot confirm it since I cannot sense the beat of her heart, I must capitalize on this opportunity. I must keep her talking, so I can remain in her presence.

"The weather is cold. I do not like it," I tell her, following Jay and Talia's advice.

She shakes her head, her gaze dreamy. "Me neither. I'm not ready for winter. Autumn is the most beautiful time of year, but it seems like it's over now."

The heat between us is hypnotic, and my breathing turns ragged as the distance between us starts to disappear. Then I briefly wonder if this is what humans experience when I use my powers on them. It would be impossible to look away from this magnificent creature even if the building were on fire. I take a step closer. "I am planning to get a pet of my own, but I do not know what kind I would be best suited for. Can you assist me with that, Harper?"

Her body moves slightly toward mine, her chest lightly brushing against my stomach, sending an electric jolt down my spine. "Cats are, um, good." I feel the tips of her heavy breasts harden beneath her clothing, and my cock pulses against my thigh. The scent that fills the room changes slightly. It is Harper's scent, but richer and heady. This must be her arousal.

She wants me. "Do not go to dinner tonight with that male. The one who was here earlier. You shall eat dinner with me instead."

Harper jerks back, the heat between us extinguished in an instant. "Excuse me?"

"He is not the one for you," I explain. "It is not safe. There is something deeply sinister about him."

"Are you serious? You don't even know him."

"Yes, I am quite serious. I would not joke about such things."

Harper adjusts the white jacket she wears, pulling it over her chest, and puts a hand on her hip. "Thanks for your concern, but who I eat dinner with is none of your business." She steps to the right and gestures to the lobby. "I think it's time for you to go. And don't come back without a pet."

"Very well," I say with a defeated nod. "Lovely to see you again, Dr. O'Connor."

She is angry at my words. I have come to understand that humans do not have the same senses as draxilios and cannot tell when a person's intentions are bad. Harper will not learn of the male's true nature until he shows it to her. I will not allow this to happen, however. I know where and when they will meet this night, and I shall be there. Until then, I must find myself a cat.

# CHAPTER 6

## HARPER

"*H*e looks like, if Colin Farrell and a Greek god had a baby," Eliza says to Ryan, describing Luka.

Ryan gasps as he cleans up the surgical suite. "Girl, get the fuck out of here."

"He's not *that* hot," I add, lying. He is precisely that hot, if not more so. "Plus, he's creepy. I don't even know how he figured out where I work. Then he has the nerve to tell me who to date. That I shouldn't go to dinner with that Colin guy. Absolutely not."

"Mmm, Colin is also wicked hot. Not as hot as Luka, but still yummy," Eliza adds.

"You went from being a depressed divorcée watching boring documentaries and *Lost* reruns every weekend, to having two straight hotties ask you out on the same day," Ryan points out. "Give yourself some time to enjoy that."

He makes watching documentaries and *Lost* reruns sound like a bad thing. "Have you seen every *Lost* episode only once? How do you expect to pick up on all the clues?"

Eliza just shakes her head disapprovingly.

"And my documentaries are boring, really?" I ask, putting finger quotes around the word boring. "That thing I shared last week about coffin birth, remember that? Where do you think I learned that?" Before they can reply, I add, "That's right, from a documentary."

Eliza groans. "Okay, I'll concede that the coffin birth discussion was morbid in an impressive way, but I also could've gone my entire life without learning about it."

"Coffin birth?" Ryan asks. "What is that? How did I miss that conversation?"

"Don't look it up," Eliza cautions him. "Seriously, don't."

"Anyway, I like my boring life and my nerdy interests, and I'm not giving them up just because a couple of good-looking guys asked me out."

"What are you wearing on your date tonight?" Ryan asks.

I mentally scan through the options currently hanging in my closet. There aren't many. Most of my "going out clothes" are low-rise flares and tube tops from two summers ago, and a couple bubble-hem dresses that I hate wearing. "There's the black dress I wore to my uncle Gerry's funeral, but maybe I can add that wide pink belt to make it more fun."

"What about the cropped vest and white tank top you wore to the club?" Eliza suggests.

"You want me to wear a tank top on a date in November? I'll look ridiculous."

Eliza scoffs as she shuts off the lights in the lobby. "You will not. He'll like that you're showing some skin." When she returns to the back room, her gaze lands on Ryan. "Ryan, you're the deciding vote here. Tank top with cropped vest: yay or nay?"

"Oh, so just because I'm gay, you think I have fashion advice to give?" he says, dropping the box of surgical masks onto the table in front of him.

Eliza and I exchange a look of panic and shout no at the same time. I adore Ryan. The last thing I'd ever want to do is insult him with a harmful stereotype.

Ryan lets out a sly chuckle and says, "I'm just kidding. But also not kidding because I've never seen your closet, doc, so I don't know what the alternatives are."

Eliza claps her hands in excitement. "Ooh, wear one of those boring, corporate conference button-downs under the vest. That'll be a good balance of sexy and classy."

Hmm. Now that she's said it, I almost can't believe that combo hadn't occurred to me. "Thank you, guys," I say, genuinely grateful for their help. "I'm nervous about this date, but also excited."

The two of them finish cleaning up the back room and offer to drive me home. I decline as I still have charts to write up from today's appointments. Before the back door to the clinic closes behind them, they yell, "Good luck tonight. Have fun."

Even though I haven't been on a first date in six years, I'm optimistic about tonight. It will be fun.

* * *

I was so, so wrong. This date is a disaster. Colin talks with his mouth full, gave me a very judgmental look when I reached for the free basket of bread, and his favorite topic of conversation seems to be…trophy hunting. This guy started out a solid nine and a half in terms of hotness, and has since plummeted to a three, and that's being generous.

"Have you ever been hunting?" he asks. This is the first question he's asked me all night, and he's not going to like the answer.

"Me? No," I reply in a flat tone as I push a broccoli stem around my plate with a fork. "It kind of goes against everything I stand for, to be honest."

Colin looks at me, surprise evident on his face, as if we didn't meet in the veterinary clinic where I spend my days healing animals. "Huh, that's a shame," he says, the hunk of steak he's still chewing on in full view as his teeth rip it apart. "Although you probably wouldn't be very good at it anyway. You have to be stealthy in the woods when you're hunting," he points his fork at me, "and you'd probably make a lot of noise hobbling around with that cane."

"Right. Sure," I mumble as my eyes roll all the way back into my head.

He nods as if he didn't notice my mood shift. "Yeah, you have to be dead silent out there. You know, blend into nature. That's the whole point." Grease from the steak forms in the corners of his mouth, my stomach turning at the sight. "Oh man, you should've seen my top kill from last year. The day was almost ruined when I tripped over a stray branch and fell on my ass, but five minutes later, this huge moose comes strolling out from behind a cluster of trees, then *boom,* I got him right between the eyes."

"Cool."

I empty my glass of wine and wonder if I should just go ahead and order an entire bottle. *Just need to get through it,* I tell myself. *Be polite and get through it, and then you can go home alone. You'll never ever have to see the inside of this asshole's mouth again.*

He clearly doesn't care what I have to say, which means I could say just about anything right now and he probably wouldn't even hear me.

"I was watching this documentary recently about whale hunting," I explain, "and it was devastating how they would separate the adult whales from their calves."

"Oh, man, whale hunting?" Colin replies, his eyes lighting up with excitement. So much for that theory. "I would love to go whale hunting." He leans toward me and lowers his voice. "How do they do it?"

He wants tips?

"With a machine gun?" he presses.

"Is that…" I trail off, wondering if he's messing with me. "Is that a serious question?" Does he think people really hunt whales with machine guns? That's my fault though, since I didn't ask him any personal questions before agreeing to go out with him. He came into the clinic with his dog and didn't seem like a complete monster, so I said yes. The next guy I go on a date with is going to get grilled like a kebab.

"What did you say you did for a living?" I ask, bracing myself for the answer.

He lifts his chin, looking way too smug for someone with meat grease on his chin. "I work for RCC."

I stare at him blankly.

"You know, Revere Creek Capital? That new VC firm."

Of course, he's what Ryan and Eliza would call "a finance bro." Just perfect.

For good measure, I look around the restaurant for Ashton Kutcher and his signature trucker hat, but nope, this isn't a prank. It's real life. Maybe I should just stay single.

It takes Colin forever to finish his meal, but eventually, the plates are cleared, and our server returns. I wince at the possibility of him wanting dessert, but before the server inquires, he says, "No dessert for us. We'll just take the check."

Is he having a terrible time too? He seems woefully unaware of what a crappy couple we'd make, so the fact that he's in a hurry to leave surprises me. "Not a dessert person?" I ask.

"Nah, I'm not into empty calories," he says, patting his flat stomach. "Nothing tastes as good as a six-pack feels. Know what I mean?"

Jesus. "I can honestly say that I don't. I've never had a six-pack."

If things weren't bad enough, he makes a big show of reaching for the check, adding, "I got this one. I know how to treat a woman," as if he's some kind of catch. If he expects me to bow at his feet for treating me to a terrible dinner, he's going to be disappointed.

Once we step outside, it's nearly impossible to conceal my excitement that I'll soon be rid of this guy. We make it to the edge of the parking lot when he places his hand on the small of my back and pulls me against his body.

Panicked, I push against his chest. "No!" I shout, but he grips me tighter, then puts a hand over my mouth, shushing me, as he hauls me into a dark alley.

"Now that we have a little privacy," he says in a low voice as he takes his hand away from my mouth and leans down for a kiss.

Instead of taking the opportunity to scream bloody murder, I lift the steel handle of my cane and shove it into his long, straight nose. His hands fly to his face as he throws his head back, moaning in pain. "Uptight bitch!"

I stumble backward until I'm back on the sidewalk, my chest heaving as I process what just happened, and what almost could've happened. A sob catches in my throat, and I stand there, frozen in fear as tears stream down my face. I should be running away. Why aren't my legs moving?

Blood pours from Colin's nose, but when he dips his chin, his gaze turns murderous as it lands on me. I suck in a breath as he launches himself forward, but before he can grab me, I'm shoved to the left, not enough to fall over, but enough to get me out of the way as a massive shadowy figure surges forward and lifts Colin a foot off the ground.

"She said no," the mysterious man says with a menacing growl.

A nearby streetlamp flickers, casting light on a crop of dirty-blond hair and a jawline that could cut glass, and I realize the shadowy figure is Luka, and his hand is wrapped around Colin's throat.

# CHAPTER 7

## LUKA

*D*espite my lack of human social skills, it is clear that Harper is having an awful time on her dinner date. Seated four tables behind Harper and this Colin fellow, I hear everything, and relief washes over me each time she responds to him in a clipped, uninterested tone. Harper is seated with her back to me, and I made sure to wear attire that would help me blend in, a blue hat with a red B on it, a pair of fake eyeglasses, and a flannel shirt. Apart from my height, I look like every other male in here.

Everything about Harper's behavior and demeanor indicates she cannot stand Colin, and when they pay their food bill and leave, I am close behind, ready to step in and wow her with all the new topics Talia suggested when I spoke with her this afternoon: the simple pleasure of a rainy day, the enjoyment I feel whenever I go shopping, and how much I admire the group of men who hit balls with bats and wear the red socks. I do not know who they are, but Talia said that Harper will be thrilled to hear of my loyalty to them.

I am trying to decide which to discuss first when I notice Colin placing his hand on Harper's lower back. A growl rumbles in my chest. He dares to touch what is mine.

*End him,* my draxilio demands.

Though I agree with him, I cannot exactly rip the limbs off this human in such a public place. The moment I see him pull Harper against his body, and her attempt to push him away, I dismiss my previous decision and decide that no matter where I obliterate this male, he shall deserve every moment of pain.

Harper manages to escape his grasp by hitting him in the nose with her cane, a scene that makes my chest swell with pride. My mate is a fighter. She does not need me to defend her honor, but I shall do so anyway because it is what she deserves.

Colin charges toward my mate, but I block his path and lift him by his fragile, wobbly neck.

"She said no," I growl, enjoying the way he gasps for breath.

*Squeeze*, my draxilio urges. *Squeeze until the life leaves his eyes.*

I ignore his request, however. Since I am in my flightless form, I have more control over my actions and logic guides my hand. If I were in my draxilio form, his urges would take the lead, and Colin would be dead.

Though, the fact that he put his hands on my mate and tried to force himself on her fills me with enough rage that I am inclined to keep my grip around his throat even when the veins in his neck bulge and his entire face turns an unsettling shade of red.

But what would Harper think of me upon witnessing such a violent act? She still does not know my true form, and killing a human would certainly make her suspicious if not altogether terrified of me. I cannot allow that, not when I have yet to spend quality time in her presence. So I lift Colin another inch off the ground before I toss him deeper into the alley. He lands against the wall with a groan, and his body curls in on itself as he rubs his neck.

He is not dead. I feel his pulse from where I stand. But I hope he has learned to keep his distance from my mate.

"Luka?" Harper begins and then, between panting breaths, says, "What the fuck did you do? Were you following me?"

I turn to face her and notice her entire body is shaking. I quickly remove my jacket and gently drape it around her shoulders. My heart feels as if it is being smashed into pieces as tears run down her cheeks.

I reach for one, catching it before it reaches her chin, then stroke across her delicate cheekbone. "I did what needed to be done...to protect you."

Backing away from me, Harper shouts, "I didn't ask you to protect me!"

"You did not need to," I tell her, lowering my voice to what I hope is a calming tone. Shoving my hands into my pockets, I take a small step forward, desperate to close the distance between us. I want nothing more than to hold her in my arms, but I do not think my touch would be welcome. "My body was made to keep you safe, Harper. I am a shield to protect you from harm. Use me."

She sighs heavily as she pulls my jacket tighter around her body. She looks so tired, my poor mate. "What are you, a professional body-guard or something?"

I did not realize that was a job one could have. I nod, thinking of Axil's words from the other day. *If a human suggests something, agree with them. As long as it does not expose what we are, let them think they know our situation. Humans are more comfortable with their own version of reality than the truth.*

"Yes," I tell her. "And, uh, I do not have a current assignment, so I am available to assist you."

"I don't need a bodyguard," she replies, her bottom lip wobbling slightly as her eyes fill with tears. Harper may not need a bodyguard, but she does need me. She just has not realized it yet.

"May I walk you home, at least?" I offer. "It is cold and dark, and you are alone."

She scrubs a hand down her face. "Fine." We take two steps before she stops and tugs on the sleeve of my shirt. "But if you try anything, I'm going to shove this cane so far down your throat that it'll come out your ass. Understand me?"

I hold up two hands in surrender as I try not to look amused by her threat. "I understand."

We walk for ten minutes in silence. I wish to say something, many things in fact, but her head is too heavy with what happened tonight for normal conversation, so I do not push it. "This is my street," she points out when we turn a corner. Then, "So who else have you worked for?"

I am puzzled by her words. "Worked for?"

"Yeah, as a bodyguard," she clarifies. "Anyone famous?"

I decide to use my previous role on Sufoi as an answer, with some crucial revisions. "I worked for a prominent political leader. My job was to eliminate anyone who aimed to cause him harm. That job lasted many years." It is not exactly true, but as one of the king's assassins, I did eliminate all threats to his safety, just in a more proactive way.

Harper's eyes sparkle with interest. "Wow, so you must have seen some crazy shit."

"I have, yes," I reply, this time with complete honesty.

"Well, this is me," she says, stopping in front of a modest, narrow two-level structure in a faded white color with multiple entry doors. She hands me my jacket, and I take it reluctantly.

"I can stay and keep an eye on you, if you would like."

"Thanks, but I'll be okay," she says.

My stomach twists with unease. I know I will have to leave her now when every cell in my body is determined to remain at her side. This has gone well, though. Harper is beginning to trust me. I hold out my hand. "Give me your phone." When she does not, I add, "Please?"

She rolls her eyes, but a smirk tugs at one side of her mouth as she places her phone in my palm, and I feel victorious. Flipping open her phone, I use the numbered buttons to enter my name the way Jay showed me, and then add my phone number before handing it back to her. "Anytime you need me, just call. It does not matter what time it is. I will come."

Her brow lifts as she takes the phone from my hands, her fingers lightly brushing against mine. A hint of her arousal scent hits my nose, and my body urges me forward.

My draxilio very much wants this too. *Take her. Fill her. Claim her.*

Again, I ignore my burning desire, knowing Harper is tired and weary from the events of the evening. She needs rest, and I will never place my needs above hers. "Goodnight, Harper," I say with a slight bow before turning away from her beautiful face and heading in the direction of home. Someday, I hope the space I call home has Harper in it, but for now, at least she knows I am close by.

My brothers are spread out on our large sectional couch when I return home, watching *The Office*, a show that Mylo has recently deemed his favorite. They chuckle in unison when the male in charge does something foolish, and do not even turn their heads to greet me. "Hey, I need your help," I say, loud enough that it gets their attention. "We need to find a cat I can claim as a pet. First, I must deal with the male that attempted to harm my mate tonight."

"Someone tried to hurt her?" Axil asks, rising to his feet. In addition to his keen observational skills, Axil enjoys a good physical altercation, and I can tell he is preparing for one now, as he cracks his knuckles. "Where do we find him?"

"No, you four will look for a cat while I deal with him on my own," I tell them. "I am not going to hurt this male. I am simply going to convince him that he wants nothing to do with Harper and will forget that she exists by the time he wakes. Then I shall meet you to continue the cat search."

"Why are we trying to find a cat?" Kyan asks with a furrowed brow. "I am not interested in caring for a pet."

"The cat will live here, but I will be responsible for its needs." When Kyan's scowl deepens, I add, "This is a crucial step to winning over my mate. It is not up for discussion."

I hear a groan and a couple sighs, but they get off the couch and follow me out the door, so that is all that matters.

"Where are we supposed to find this cat?" Mylo asks as we make our way down the alley behind our building. "Is there only one kind? How will we know if the first one we discover is the right one?"

"Cats are small and furry, have pointed ears, and walk on four tiny paws," I explain. "I do not care what kind of cat it is. The first one we find will be the right one. Now, I must go, but I shall return shortly."

"Ah, like the one in the cartoon," Mylo says to the rest of my brothers. "The cartoon we saw yesterday had a cat in it. Remember?"

They all nod.

With that, I climb the narrow ladder on the back of our building to our private roof deck. It is a tall building with a large doorway leading inside that I can duck behind in order to shift. But being outside in the middle of an urban area such as this makes it a risk, regardless of how well I can hide as I change forms. Hopefully, the late hour and the fact that the temperature is below freezing will cut down on the number of possible prying eyes. I must do this quickly.

Closing my eyes, I inhale deeply as I picture my draxilio with his shimmering blue scales and wide, majestic wings. That is all it takes, and I am transformed. There is no time to stretch or shake out my wings, as anyone could see me up here. Leaping into the air, my invisibility cloak is activated, and I let out a deep exhale. My mind drifts back to the strong, bitter, chemical scent of whatever liquid Colin doused himself in for his date, then I find it near the restaurant and track it from there.

The scent trail takes me to a small, single-level structure close to the large body of water that hugs the city, and I land in an empty lot two blocks away.

When I knock on the door of the small house, a frail old woman answers the door in what looks to be a wrinkled night dress. I am surprised, but I still smell Colin here, and even more so now that the door is open, so he must be here. "I am looking for Colin. Is he at home this evening?"

"Uh," she stammers, looking around in a way that indicates she is confused. "There's no one here by that name."

What? How could that be? Is she lying to cover for him? Her pulse is even, which makes me think she is not lying, but just to be certain, I lock my gaze onto hers and pull her under my influence. "You will tell me the truth, ma'am. Is there a man called Colin here?"

In a robotic voice, she answers, "No, there is no one here by that name."

Frustrated, I release the old woman from my trance and thank her for her time before I depart. I am frustrated and perplexed by the conflicting information. His scent was thick, yet the woman spoke honestly when she said he was not there. As I return to the empty lot and shift into my draxilio, I decide to handle Colin tomorrow. Perhaps I shall track him from his place of business.

But first, I must find a cat.

When I land on our roof and shift into my flightless form, the phone in my back pocket beeps incessantly.

> Jay: At TB with the bros. Come get some grub.

They are at Taco Bell? Why? How? I gave them explicit instructions to look for a cat. After leaving Harper's clinic, I went to Jay's shop and asked him to show me a picture of a cat. Then I spent the entire afternoon walking around the city looking for such a creature, and I found nothing. My body grows tired. I need this taken care of soon, so I have a reason to see my mate tomorrow.

I meet Jay and my brothers in the parking lot, my eyes drifting to the bag of food slung over Zev's arm and the small paper cup in his hand. "What is that?" I ask, pointing to the cup.

Instead, he holds up the bag. "I got you three burritos. You are hungry, yes?"

"No, I am not," I say with a groan. "What happened to finding me a cat?"

Mylo smiles widely. "It is not an easy task, brother. That is what the milk is for." He points to the paper cup Zev is holding.

I do not understand. "Milk?"

"All right, I need to wait for Talia. She's closing up now. G'night, boys," Jay says with a wave as he goes back to the restaurant.

Zev approaches, his face alight with optimism. "It is for the cat. Cats like milk, so the milk will lure them to us."

This seems like an odd plan. A flimsy one too. Unless cats have exceptional noses, they will not be able to smell a small cup of milk halfway across the city. And if the cat I seek can only smell from short distances, then we do not need the milk to find the cat.

"Do not worry, brother," Mylo pipes in. "We saw it on the cartoon."

I look at Axil and Kyan hoping they will insert some logic or provide a biting retort of some kind. They both shrug. "Nothing else has worked," Axil says.

I rub my forehead, then gesture for my brothers to follow me. "Let us retire. I did not realize it would be this difficult to find a cat. Jay made it seem like available cats were all over the city. Come. I shall try again tomo—"

A faint sound I do not recognize stops me in my tracks. It is the cry of an animal, but it is labored and faint, and it comes from the alley directly to our right. Putting a finger to my lips, I lead my brothers down the darkened alley until we are standing next to a dumpster. I hear the mewling cry once more, and I follow it to the narrow space behind the dumpster where there is a dirty, fur-covered creature with a flat face, only three legs, and goo oozing from its closed left eye, lying on a pile of papers.

"Is that..." Kyan starts, his face twisted in disgust. "Is that a cat? Are they supposed to look like that?"

"Yes, brother," I reply, with a wide grin. He, or she, is just what I need. "That is a cat."

Axil grunts. "It smells vile. Perhaps we should find a different cat."

"No," I protest. "This one is perfect." When I lean down to reach for it, my new pet slashes its grimy claws down my face.

# CHAPTER 8

## LUKA

"*Y*ou are being quite foolish, brother," Zev says as we enter our apartment. "Surely you must see that."

I look down at the cat's dirty front claws that are stuck in my forearm and nod. "Perhaps, but I wanted a cat and we found one." The cat continues to buck and hiss in my arms, and the moment the front door is closed, I ease into a crouch, and it jumps from my arms before scampering down the hall.

Kyan sidles up next to me and inspects my wound. It is bleeding and the skin around it is an angry shade of red, but it will heal soon enough. "You should clean that. I do not know what diseases dumpster cats carry, but I would assume that one has contracted all of them."

I toe off my boots by the door and head into my private bathroom. This cat does look diseased, but I am confident that our superior healing abilities will fight off any infections before they develop. Still, the creature looks as if it has not encountered soap in a century, so I scrub the torn skin on my forearm just to be safe.

"Luka!" Mylo shouts from the living room seconds before I hear glass breaking. I press a towel over my wound as I race toward the commotion.

Sliding into the room on socked feet, I spot a shattered pint glass on the wood floor in front of the TV stand, the contents of which are splattered on the shag rug beneath the coffee table. Luckily, the beverage was orange juice, and the color matches the rug.

"Your foul feline just knocked my drink over," Kyan says through gritted teeth. His eyes dart around the couch. "And now it is defecating on the floor!"

The putrid scent hits my nose and the five of us groan in disgust.

"I am not cleaning that," Axil grumbles with his arms crossed as he stomps toward his bedroom.

I do not blame him. Whatever it is that is currently passing through the cat's body is a mess of varying colors and consistencies, and cleaning the floor, and the cat as well, will be deeply unpleasant tasks. It was my choice to bring the cat here, so it is my responsibility to clean up after it. "It is fine. I shall deal with this."

Zev hands me a roll of paper towels and a pair of rubber cleaning gloves. He puts on a pair of his own and unfolds a large black trash bag. When I shoot him a look of surprise, he shrugs and says, "This not a solo mission. You will need assistance tidying the beast's behind."

He is right. This will not be easy. In fact, it would be best if we had some space to get this done. I think the cat would appreciate fewer bodies in here too. "Mylo, go to the store and grab more milk for the cat. Take Kyan with you."

I pull the gloves on and begin wiping the mess on the floor as they reluctantly agree and leave. The cat starts walking toward the kitchen, its behind dripping with each labored step, and I drop the paper towels. "Zev, we must clean the cat first. We can do this after."

My brother and I end up in staring battle for several seconds, silently begging the other to reach for the cat, until I admit defeat. "Fine. But if it runs, you must help me catch it."

He nods reluctantly, his lips curling as another wave of the cat's stench hits us. "Deal."

Before it can scurry out of the room, I gently wrap my hands around its rib cage and hold it as far from my body as possible as I carry it toward my bathroom. Zev keeps pace at my side, pressing a folded paper towel against the cat's bottom. I hold the cat firmly as I place it in the sink, and Zev makes quick work of soaping up its rear and scrubbing it gently with warm water. The cat hisses and swings its front claws at me the entire time, but I am getting better at dodging them. We do not attempt to give the creature a full bath, as that would take hours due to the layers of grime and gook that cover its body. This will have to do for now.

"Now what?" Zev asks with a huff as he finishes drying the cat's rear.

I don't have a place to put the cat while we clean the mess it left on the floor, so I suppose we have no choice but to let it roam freely until we are done. At least it will not be leaving a stinky mess in its wake anymore. "Go shut the doors to the bedrooms apart from mine. Then we can let it walk around."

The cat meows loudly in my arms when Zev leaves the room, and I wonder if it prefers the company of my brother to me. "Too bad," I tell it. "You are mine now. We must find a way to coexist."

A hiss is the only response I get.

When Zev returns, I put the cat down and it runs out of my bathroom and jumps awkwardly onto my bed. For an animal with only three legs, it moves around better than I expected.

I nod toward the living room. "Okay, let us finish this."

We work together swiftly and silently as we scrub the floor, first removing the pile of waste it left for us, and then the shattered glass. Zev is spraying the rug with carpet cleaner when my phone rings. I rip my gloves off before pulling it out of my back pocket.

"Mylo?" I answer. "What is it?"

"We need your help," he says, his voice cloaked with shame. "We, uh, did something quite stupid."

I let out a weary sigh. "What now?"

"Just come to the Food Mart on the corner. Now."

The call disconnects, and I roughly run my hand through my hair. "Axil!" I yell.

He emerges from his room with his signature scowl.

"Come with me to the Food Mart. Mylo and Kyan have gotten themselves into trouble."

Zev chuckles. "What did they do?"

"They did not say. Something stupid, but they did not specify."

Axil rolls his eyes. "That is hardly surprising."

I stop in my tracks and whirl around to face him with a heated glare. "As if you have not taken part in their rascality? Have you forgotten the time we were thrown out of the lunch buffet because you and Kyan were eating soup directly from the serving stations?"

Blood rushes to Axil's cheeks as he dips his gaze to the floor. "Right. Well that was–"

"Or the time you tried to use an expired coupon for laundry soap to buy the little electronic music box?"

Axil tilts his head. "Music box? You mean iPod?"

I throw up my hands. "Whatever! You could not just apologize for your mistake. You had to demand the store employee honor it, and now we can never return."

"In fairness," Zev says in a quiet voice, "we thought the 'Buy One, Get One Free' deal could be applied to anything in the store."

"It had a picture of the laundry soap right on it," I snap back.

Axil opens his mouth to say something, but I have lost my patience entirely.

"Just come along. We need to get Mylo and Kyan."

He follows, keeping a safe distance behind me as we ride the elevator down to the first floor and walk up the street to the Food Mart. Mylo and Kyan are standing inside the doorway of the store, their clothes wet and dripping as the store clerk shouts at them. It is not until I see the empty milk containers flattened on the floor that I understand what has occurred.

"There you are," Mylo says with a relieved sigh.

"These two were trying to steal from me," the clerk yells. He is a short man with a red face and only a few wisps of white hair surround his ears. His faded long-sleeve shirt has a racecar on it, and his pants are tightly belted around the bulge of his belly but loosely hanging off his legs. He holds up a large silver phone. "I am calling the police!"

"What were you thinking?" Axil asks, grabbing Kyan by the arm. I hear Mylo start to explain, but I have no interest in hearing their excuses. I need to stop this from escalating any further.

"Sir, I beg of you not to contact the authorities," I plead. Pulling out my wallet, I drop four twenty paper bills on the counter. "I can assure you this will not happen again. Can this serve as proper restitution?"

I am not above using my influence to convince him to forget this ever happened, but my brothers are at fault here, and unless he does contact the police, I see no need to do so.

He slaps his palm on the counter and crumples the money in his clenched fist. Lifting it to my face, he says, "I never want to see them in here. Or you! You are banned. Every last one of you."

I apologize to the clerk a few times before I lead my brothers out of the store. They remain silent on the walk home. I am so angry I want to shift and singe the hair off their heads, but the crowded city street is no place for such antics. This is something they still do not seem to grasp, however, and that makes my blood boil. "You smell awful," I say without turning to look at them. "Worse than the cat, in fact."

"There is no universe in which that can be true," Kyan replies in a snide tone.

I turn on my heel and he bumps into my chest. "Explain yourself. Now."

He steps back and sighs. "We got the milk you requested, but we quickly realized that we both forgot our wallets."

"So you thought stealing the milk was the best course of action to take?"

Mylo leans in, his clothes emitting a sour odor, and says, "You steal from people all the time, brother."

"That is different," I tell him. "The ones I steal from are terrible, and they have so much money they probably do not even notice the amount that we take from them." The shocked expressions of the passersby tells me I should lower my voice. Quieter, I say, "They also do not notice my thievery while it is occurring, and with my influence, even if they remember me, they will recall giving me the money willingly. What you attempted tonight was different, and you know that."

"We thought we could make it back to the apartment before the clerk even realized what happened," Kyan adds.

I look down at their wet clothes. "Clearly you were wrong about that."

Mylo gives Kyan a pointed glare. "Yes, well, I did not expect my co-conspirator to trip me the moment we decided to make a quick exit."

Kyan turns on Mylo and gets in his face. "You tripped yourself! My foot just happened to be in front of you at the time. Perhaps you should look where you are going from now on."

"So you tripped, both of you, and fell on top of the milk you were trying to steal?" Axil asks with a smirk that he is not even trying to hide.

"You should have called me and asked me to bring you some money," I tell them. I do not enjoy scolding them as if they are children, but this is just embarrassing. On top of this, I have a cat at home that is clearly unhealthy and does not like me at all.

"We are sorry," Mylo finally says with his head hung low. Kyan stays silent until Mylo elbows him in the ribs.

"Sorry," Kyan grunts. "Truly. We did not think it would turn out like this." He gestures to his milk-covered clothes, and my rage softens, but only a little.

"Go home," I tell them when we turn onto our street. "I will meet you there."

"Where are you going?" Mylo asks.

I pick up my pace and yell over my shoulder, "To get the milk I trusted you two to get."

My milk purchase goes smoothly and without incident, and I walk the two blocks home as fast my legs will take me. I have no idea what I am returning home to, and that twists my stomach into knots. Has the cat pooped again? Or broken any more glass? Has it scratched the ignorant smirks off Kyan and Mylo's faces? That I would not mind, actually.

The apartment is quiet when I close and lock the front door behind me. I appreciate the space it seems my brothers have chosen to give me. My bones ache and my mind is reeling from the events of the day. I want nothing more than to feed this cat and go to sleep. The sooner I fall asleep, the sooner I will see my mate once more.

I picture her face as I pour the milk into a small ceramic bowl for the cat. Will she be pleased to see me again? And with a cat in my arms? Will she need to spend the entire day treating the many ailments of my new pet? Perhaps she will grow so attached to the creature that she will ask if she can come over and help it get settled into its new home.

Placing the bowl on the floor next to my bed, I watch as the cat flops down onto the floor and starts lapping it up with its tongue. I remove my clothes and change into loose shorts before going into the bathroom to rinse my face and brush my teeth.

A strange hacking sound has me racing from the bathroom back into my bedroom, where I find the cat sitting in the middle of my bed, vomiting onto my freshly laundered sheets.

It is far too late, and I am too tired to summon anger at my new roommate, so I grab the down comforter off the bed, along with one of the pillows, and admit defeat as I lay down on the floor. "The bed is yours tonight, cat. Tomorrow, we shall reassess our arrangement."

# CHAPTER 9

## HARPER

*T*his might be the busiest Thursday the clinic has ever had. I went from back-to-back exams to three surgeries, took a five-minute break to shove a turkey wrap down my throat, and then back to appointments. I thought I had a bit of a break following my two o'clock appointment with the golden retriever who had an ear infection, but the moment that client leaves, another is put into the exam room next to it.

"Hottie with a body and a hot mess cat he found next to a dumpster in room three," Eliza says with a wink as she passes me in the hall.

Next to a dumpster? I pull the chart from its shelf outside the door and can't help but smile when I see Luka's name. When did he adopt a cat? He didn't have one yesterday afternoon, and I saw him again last night when he saved me from Colin, the handsy dipshit, as Ryan has renamed him.

Through the door, I hear the cat hissing at him, and Luka whispering, "Do *not* do that again. I am serious this time."

"Well hello there," I greet as I step into the room.

The cat is wrapped in a towel and sits on the exam table in the middle of the room, its tail swishing back and forth angrily. Luka is huddled in the back corner, wearing a wrinkled red T-shirt that seems a size too big and dark jeans that have more than one mysterious stain. His hair is messier than I've seen it previously, and he looks exhausted. There are scratches all over his face and hands, and whenever he reaches for the cat, he's met with an angry hiss.

"Aww, who's this little floof?" I ask as I enter the room. It's a Persian cat, with its signature flat nose and big eyes, its fur is mostly white except for a black splotch on its front left foot, making it appear as if he or she is wearing one black sock. It also has only three legs. The cat stops hissing when it sees me, and I notice the poor thing has a severe eye infection.

"It is my cat. I do not know if it is male or female, however," Luka says, crossing his arms over his chest.

After giving it a scratch behind its ear, it rolls over on its belly for me, a sign of trust. "Congrats, it's a boy, and he's already neutered, so that's good."

Luka steps forward and sticks his hand out, but when the cat notices, he goes right back to hissing.

"He's nicer to you at home, I hope?" I ask, brushing the back of my fingers against the stray's cheek. He lets out a loud, contented purr and pushes against my hand.

"No, he hates me." Luka chuckles, the sound low and raspy. Then he shakes his head in awe. "But he seems completely bewitched by you...and that, I understand."

My belly flutters at his words. I just hope my cheeks aren't as red as they feel. I'm still skeptical of Luka's intentions, but I have to admit, the guy is growing on me. He's weird, and there's a chance he's been stalking me, but I don't feel uncomfortable around him. If anything, when he's near me, I've never felt safer.

Maybe I'm just terrible at reading people. Colin is certainly proof of that, but part of me wants to give Luka a chance. He did save me from Colin, after all.

"What's this little guy's name?" I ask, shifting the focus back to the patient where it should be.

Luka frowns. "He does not have a name. He is a cat."

"Whaaat?" Ryan says as he enters the room. "Every cat has a name."

I let out a breath, relieved we're no longer alone. His beauty is a distraction. "Luka, this is our head technician, Ryan. Ryan, this is Luka."

"Nice to meet you, sir," Ryan greets, giving Luka a nod. Then Ryan carefully lowers his hand near where I'm petting the cat, to gauge his aggression. The cat doesn't hiss, and when Luka notices, a muscle in his jaw ticks. "Nice to meet you too, little buddy," Ryan says to the cat.

Ryan gets into position, keeping a gentle hold on the cat while I press my stethoscope to the cat's heart, then listen to his lungs. Once that's done, I examine the inside of his ears, skin, and the spot where his fourth leg was amputated, then I get a closer look at the cat's infected eye.

"Okay, so our boy here needs a lot of care," I begin, gesturing for Luka to join us at the exam table. I separate a clump of fur near the cat's neck. "He's covered in fleas, and I see quite a few patches of dry, irritated skin. We can take care of that with a bath and flea preventative, though it may take a few weeks for the fleas to die off completely. We can also shave down the knots in his fur because I'm sure those are bothering him.

"His heartbeat is strong, but he sounded a bit congested when I listened to his lungs, so I'd like to get him x-rayed in order to rule out pneumonia, then we can get him started on an oral antibiotic." Luka's eyes widen in terror, so I quickly add, "Don't worry, you can just put it in his food. I'd also like to send you home with a topical antibiotic for his eye," I continue, using a piece of gauze to wipe away the crusty secretions that have pinched his eye shut.

The cat continues to purr even as I poke and prod him. Such a little sweetheart. "We'll do a cytology to determine the kind of infection he has and give you the best medication for it."

"What about his missing leg?" Luka asks. "Does that need to be addressed?"

"Actually, no," I tell him, getting the cat to lay on his back again, so I can show him the amputation scar where the back left leg used to be. "I would guess he wasn't always a stray. The leg was removed surgically, and he seems to have healed nicely. He's probably gotten used to not having it, but we can get him on a joint supplement that will make it easier for him to move around."

"Wow, I did not realize having a cat would be so much work," Luka says, rubbing the back of his neck.

"Well, when you find a cat living by a dumpster, it's safe to assume they aren't thriving." The cat throws himself down on his side, into my hand, begging for more scratches. I let out a giggle as I give in to the little guy's demands. "He's lucky you found him."

Luka straightens his spine, his heated gaze locked on me. "Whatever he needs, I shall provide it." His words, along with his steady gaze, make it sound like a vow he would never break, and for a moment I wonder if he's talking about the cat.

"Um," I mutter, trying to ignore the squeeze of my core around nothing, and how, for the first time in years, it's an emptiness I want filled. "Do you need us to send home some cat food? Or do you already have some?"

"I should get some," he says. "I bought a carton of milk last night, but I do not know how long it will last."

"Milk?" I ask, startled by his comment. "You've been giving him milk?"

"Yes."

"And he's been keeping it down?"

"Well, no," Luka admits. "He vomited on my bed in the middle of the night."

I chuckle because the mental image of that, and what I imagine to be Luka's subsequent reaction, is hilarious. "Yeah, most cats are actually lactose intolerant, so stop giving him milk."

He drops his head into his hands. "Ugh, I have been tripping over my own tail."

It's an odd phrase I've never heard anyone use, but from context, I can tell that Luka is upset. Instinctively, I sidle up to him and put a comforting hand on his shoulder. "It's not your fault, really. Cartoons lied to us. A lot of people assume milk is safe for cats because of that."

His head snaps up to stare at my hand, which has begun rubbing small circles into his shoulder of its own accord, and I drop it to my side in a panic. What the hell am I doing, pawing at a client?

"Um, Ryan, why don't you take this sweet baby to the back, so we can get started on treatment?"

"You got it, doc," Ryan replies with a nod, softly pulling the cat into his arms and leaving the room.

My phone buzzes in my pocket, and when I see who it is, I roll my eyes and put it back where it was. "Sorry, I, um…" I trail off, unsure if I'm apologizing for the interruption, the clear line I crossed when I touched him, or my general lack of focus. "I'm going to head back too, so I can get the cytology running." I go to leave, but then I remember a crucial step that almost slipped my mind. "Would you like a treatment plan first, so you can see what today's visit will cost?"

"Not necessary," Luka quickly replies. "I have the funds for whatever he needs." Then he puts a hand over his heart. "Thank you for your help today."

Okay, the combination of manners, gratitude, and confidence that he can afford whatever it costs to care for his cat is making me clench my thighs together.

"I'll be back with him soon," I tell Luka before scurrying out of the room and into the small bathroom at the end of the hall. I splash my face with cold water and give myself a hard look in the mirror. Enough drooling over this guy. Once I feel like I've regained my composure, I meet Ryan in the treatment area of the back room and get to work.

It takes almost an hour to get Luka's cat bathed, shaved, x-rayed, and for the cytology to give me the results I need. Ryan carries the cat, whom he lovingly calls *Viper* because when he was shaving a section of knotted fur, the cat took a quick and aggressive swipe at Ryan's wrist, which is now wrapped in a bandage. We enter the room together, and Luka gasps at the sight of his new pet all cleaned up.

"He does not even look like the ball of dirt I found."

Ryan and I laugh. "Nope, he's in much better shape now," I tell him. Then I explain the x-rays and how there is no sign of pneumonia, the cytology results, and the medications Luka needs to give the cat in order to treat both the eye and lung infections. "He'll be even better in a week or two once he's on a healthy diet and the medications start working their magic."

Ryan clears his throat. "This is entirely your call, of course, but what about the name *Viper*?"

Luka's eyes drop to the fresh bandage on Ryan's wrist, and he laughs quietly. The way his dark gray eyes swirl with warmth and subtle lines form around his delectably thick lips captivates me. "That is indeed the perfect name for him."

"Yesss," Ryan replies with a triumphant hiss.

My phone buzzes, but I don't take it out of my pocket this time. I know who it is. It's the same person who's been texting me all day. Luka eyes my pocket momentarily, but when the vibrating stops, I smile and show him the bag of food I'm sending him home with. "You'll want to give him a quarter cup twice a da—"

My phone buzzes again, but this time it's not a text. It's a phone call. I peek at the screen, and Colin's name flashes across it. "Ryan, could you be a dear and put my phone in the office?" I ask, handing it to him.

"Sure thing, doc." He takes it, but when he sees the name, he asks, "On your desk or just flush it down the toilet?"

His protective quip cheers me up, but only a little.

Once Ryan leaves, Luka takes a step in my direction. Now that Viper is in a better mood, Luka gets as close to the two of us as he can before Viper lets out a single quiet hiss. I can feel heat radiating from his body in waves. He's like a tree-sized furnace that smells of fresh laundry and cinnamon. "Harper, are you well?"

*No, but I'd feel better if you took off your shirt,* I want to say, but instead, I brush off the whole ordeal. "It's nothing. Really."

"Nothing?" he asks, eyeing me skeptically.

Biting my lip, I give in to his penetrating gaze. "It's Colin. He keeps texting me, saying he's sorry. That I should give him another chance, and we should go out again, blah, blah, blah. That was him just now, trying to call me, probably because I haven't responded to his texts."

"Good," he says in a dark tone. "He does not deserve another moment of your attention," then, under his breath, I hear, "Pitiful *joshik*."

"Uh, what?"

He shakes his head. "Nothing. I will remind you, Harper, that I am still available to serve as your bodyguard. It would be an honor."

I thank him for his offer, but once again decline. This is nothing more than an idiot with an infatuation. He tried copping a feel, and I put him in his place. Most likely, he was shocked I was able to do so with all my "hobbling around" with my cane. He sees me as hard to get, hence the pursuit. But once he gets the hint that I'm clearly not interested, he'll find someone else to annoy.

Once I show Luka how much food to give Viper, I go over how to administer the medications, and, because Luka seems like a clueless cat dad, I give him a checklist of other essentials he should have on hand to ensure Viper's comfort: a crate, litter box, litter, a cat bed, and maybe some toys for him to play with.

His fingers brush against mine as I give him the list, and I quiver at the jolt of electricity that goes straight down my spine. Panic fills my chest at the thought of him leaving. I don't want him to. The panic worsens at the realization that I'm somehow getting attached to this relative stranger. That can't happen.

When we walk out to the lobby, I notice a large bouquet of pink roses on the reception desk. "Ooh, does Eliza have a secret admirer?" I ask, teasing.

Eliza frowns, and that's when it clicks. The roses aren't for her. They're for me. Hesitantly, I reach for the card tied to the front of the vase, and my suspicions are confirmed when I turn it over. The card says, "Give me a chance to show you the man I really am. Meet me tonight for dinner at seven thirty. Faneuil Hall. You won't be disappointed. Love, Colin."

I turn to look at Luka, and his expression can only be described as *I won't say the words, but…told you so.*

"You know what?" I say, deciding to throw in the towel. "Yes, I–I think I'd like to, I mean, I need to hire you for–"

"I am at your service, Dr. O'Connor," he says with a slight bow.

"Listen, I don't want you hovering over me at all times. You may walk me to and from work, then leave after that. I can't have you distracting me while I'm seeing patients."

"What about when you are home alone?"

"I'll be fine. I have two locks on my front door, and I keep a kitchen knife next to my bed."

He stares at me as if waiting to see if I'll change my mind. What does he expect, that I'll invite him to move in with me? Not gonna happen. "Very well."

I'm concerned I'll regret this decision, but in the next moment, Viper lets out a dramatic "meeeoow" as he reaches for me with one of his front paws, and I melt where I stand. "I should be done here at seven."

"I shall be here at six forty-five to escort you home."

"Sounds good. Knock three times on the back door so I know it's you."

He pays his bill, and I can't tear my eyes from his wide back as he walks down the sidewalk with Viper squirming in his heavily muscled arms.

"So…" Eliza starts, absolutely beaming with pride, "you have a bodyguard now, huh?"

I pick up the vase full of roses and dump them in the trash. "Yep, I have a bodyguard now."

# CHAPTER 10

## HARPER

*L*uka arrives at six forty-three, knocking on the back door just as I instructed him. The clinic has been closed since six, and once everyone else left, I locked all the doors to be on the safe side. He's changed into a navy-blue button-down shirt that he's left untucked, maroon twill pants that hang at the perfect length over his functional black boots, and the same black puffy coat he wrapped around me the night before. His clothes are free of wrinkles and stains, and the scratches on his face have already faded significantly.

"You look much better than you did this morning," I tell him as I lock the door behind him.

He smiles, and it's the first time I've noticed how straight and white his teeth are. His lack of flaws is...frustrating, in a way. "A single shower can work miracles."

Stifling a moan at the image of him naked in the shower, I nervously mumble something about having to finish writing up a few charts, and that I'll be done soon. He strolls down the hall, looking around as he waits.

Once I'm done, I lock up the clinic and set the alarm. We start walking, and he quickly outpaces me. "Can we slow it down a bit?" I ask, favoring my aching knee. "I'm a little sore today."

He stops and waits for me, his gaze lingering on my cane. "Go ahead. You can ask about it."

"I do not wish to pry."

"It's okay, really," I assure him. I'm never offended by the curiosity piqued by my limp. It's only when people treat me differently that I have a problem. "I was in a bad skiing accident about five years ago. God I miss skiing. My ex-husband, Freddy, and I used to go all the time. Then, one day, I leaned slightly the wrong way, and I felt myself going off the trail, so I tried to correct, overcorrect instead, and I crashed right into a tree."

Luka listens intently. It looks like he has a hundred questions he wants to ask, but he remains quiet as I continue.

"I ended up with multiple fractures in my left leg and hip. I was lucky to survive, honestly. Not long into my recovery, I was diagnosed with osteonecrosis." When Luka shoots me a puzzled look, I say, "It's basically the death of bone tissue. I refused the cane for a while."

The memories of my recovery—the pain and anger I felt when I had to accept that my body would never be the same—are still fresh in my mind. "Eventually, I noticed how much it helped me. How much pain I was in at the end of a day when I didn't use it compared to when I did. So, my cane is always with me wherever I go. No exceptions."

"How often are you in pain?" he finally asks.

"Mmm, on a scale of one to ten, I'd say I'm always at least a four, and at night is when it's the worst. That's when I feel how much I've moved throughout the day. Some of my nights are pretty bad, a nine, nine and a half, occasionally."

He stops in his tracks, facing me. "That is atrocious. It is not fair for you to experience such consistent misery. You deserve better."

"Misery isn't the word I'd choose," I tell him honestly. I've always tried to maintain a positive attitude about my leg since so many others have it far worse, and I did survive the accident, after all. Of course, there are days when I think about all the things I can't do, and I get so angry that I take a kitchen knife to an old set of sheets and turn them into ribbons to let out the frustration.

Mostly, I've gotten used to the pain. It's part of my routine now. "I do my physical therapy exercises, I ice it every night, and take ibuprofen when the pain gets bad. On the days when I just can't walk at all, I have Ryan or Eliza pick me up and drive me to and from the clinic, and I stay in my rolling chair during exams. It's not so bad."

"Are you the only doctor employed at the clinic? What about the days when the pain is so severe you cannot tend to your patients?"

He makes a good point. "There is another doctor, Dr. Brooks—he owns the place," I tell him. "I can't rely on him much though. The few times I have called in sick, he turns it into a whole thing, and I have to listen to him complain for days after. I'd rather work through the pain."

Luka growls.

I've done the same, and I appreciate his anger on my behalf. Especially when I think about the time Dr. Brooks had a mild cold and called in sick for a week and a half. I didn't complain once when he finally returned.

"Do you have pets of your own, Harper?" Luka asks, his tone abrupt and still holding a hint of disdain.

"Not at the moment, no. I'm not unwilling to adopt a dog or cat. I guess I'm just waiting for the right one to find me," I say with a chuckle. Really, I was waiting to pull myself out of my depressed state that followed my divorce, and since that's now behind me, I could start looking. Maybe a visit to the shelter this weekend is in order...

"I must make a phone call. Wait here," he says, his hand hovering over my arm as if he wants to touch me but doesn't want me to feel uncomfortable. "Do not move."

A twisted part of my mind wants to run, just to see how he'd react. Would he chase me? What would he do when he caught me? How would it feel to be trapped in his strong arms? Since I'm more sore than usual today, I decide to fantasize about it rather than actually doing it.

I hear him whispering low into his flip phone, but I can't tell what he's saying. Eventually, he says, "Good. See you shortly," and my teeth clench at the thought of him maybe going home to someone after he walks me home. Is he married? Is he dating someone? I guess I assumed he was interested in me with the whole "hey, let's fornicate" request and the stalking that followed. Maybe I've been reading him wrong.

Luka ends the call, and we continue walking. He peppers me with more questions in that same blunt way of his that I'm starting to appreciate. It's strange, but I like that he doesn't play games. I like how open he seems. When he wants an answer to something, he simply asks a question.

He asks about my childhood, what it's like to be a veterinarian, and the conversation naturally leads to my marriage. "He did not make you happy. That is why you left him?"

"I don't think it was his fault or mine. We just grew apart, and I didn't notice it was happening until we were living completely separate lives under the same roof. Freddy continued to go on ski trips without me, and I developed other hobbies in place of that. We ended up having nothing in common. I was the one who asked for the divorce and filed the paperwork, but he wanted it to end too. I could tell."

"I do not understand divorce," he says, clasping his hands behind his back. "It seems impossible to fall out of love with the person you pledge the rest of your days to."

It's a nice thought, but a naïve one too. "If only love were as simple as that."

"It is," he says, his tone serious. Then, in a quieter voice, "Where I come from, anyway."

"Where are you from? I don't think you've told me."

"You have not asked."

Luka seems…irritated with me. Why? I mean, I guess we have spent the entire walk talking about me. Come to think of it, I haven't asked him anything. The very thing I judged Colin for, I'm doing to Luka.

"I'm sorry. You're right, I should've asked," I tell him. "Sorry."

He runs a rough hand through his hair, groaning in frustration. "There is no need for your apologies. I find certain things," he pauses as though searching for the words, "difficult to comprehend, and I grow angry with myself when they remain confusing even after they have been explained to me."

My heart squeezes at the sight of him so vulnerable in his admission. Does he think he's the only one who doesn't fully understand love? Because I certainly don't get it either. I open my mouth to say something comforting, but he cuts me off.

"I did not have a pleasant upbringing. My brothers and I, we escaped a...cult," he says with an audible swallow. "We did not have parents. We had handlers, and they did not treat us with kindness."

"My god," I say with a horrified gasp. My hand reaches for his instinctively, and once our fingers entwine, I squeeze his hand in an attempt to comfort him. "That's awful, Luka. I'm so sorry."

One side of his mouth curves up slightly, and he nods. "I thank you for that. You need not pity me, however. I shared my past with you only to help explain why I find divorce such a perplexing concept."

"Couples in your cult didn't get divorced?"

"No," he says, shaking his head. "Among my kind, love was eternal. It was clear and evident between the two people who felt it for one another, and it never wavered. Not even for a moment." He sighs heavily. "I know the place I once called home was rife with problems, but that was not one of them."

I have a hard time accepting that the cult he escaped had any positive aspects to it at all, given that he had to escape it in the first place, but I'm not about to tell him how he should feel about a traumatic situation he's still processing.

It also explains a lot about him. The way he speaks, the odd things that sometimes come out of his mouth. I wonder what it's like for him to exist in a place that is so unlike where he was raised.

"Can I ask..." I trail off, trying to find a way to say this that won't insult him. "How come you never use contractions?"

"Contractions?" he repeats with a furrow of his brow. "That is when you mash two words together?"

"Yeah."

"It simply was not done where I come from. In the, uh, the cult," he stammers, "it was considered lazy to combine words, and it would make the speaker seem as if they were rushing to get the words out if they combined any. Speaking slowly and enunciating each word was considered proper."

That's a unique way of looking at it, I guess.

We finally reach my place, and just as we do, a silver Volkswagen Beetle pulls up. A giant man, who I recognize from the night I met Luka at The Shadow Den, climbs out of the passenger seat with a plastic bag full of items slung over his arm and a black mesh pet carrier in hand.

"Ah, splendid," Luka says with a smile that lights up his entire face. "Harper, this is my brother, Axil. Axil, this is Harper."

"An honor to meet you, Harper," Axil says, shaking my hand. Then he turns to Luka. "Here you are, brother. I must say, I am looking forward to a quiet night." He winks at Luka, then waves goodbye to both of us as he climbs back in the car and it speeds off.

"What is—" I start to say.

"Viper," Luka replies, answering my question before I've even finished asking it. "Along his many medications and accessories, of course." He holds the carrier up, and the moment Viper sees my face, he starts mewing loudly.

"Hi, little man," I mutter in a pitch too high for regular human conversation.

"When you said you had no current pets, I called Axil to see if he could bring Viper to you."

My mouth falls open. It's like he read my mind.

"That is who I was speaking to on the phone earlier."

It wasn't another woman, but his brother, and he made the call for *me*.

"While I will not be here throughout the night guarding your body, I thought Viper would do a fine job of that until I arrive to walk you to work in the morning."

I don't hear anything after "guarding your body" because I'm too busy staring at his mouth. His incredible mouth, surrounded by laugh lines and neatly groomed stubble that adds an edge to his intense beauty.

*Fuck me.* I want to run my tongue all over my bodyguard.

"I'm sorry," I call out, instantly realizing I'm apologizing for the thoughts in my head that he has no knowledge of.

He tilts his head to the side and gives me a strange look. "You apologize too much."

It's the kind of astute comment I wouldn't expect from someone who is still basically a stranger. Certainly not *this* beautiful sex god.

"It is as if you believe your presence is a burden to those around you," he continues. "It is not, so stop."

That's what breaks me. His blunt, empowering compliment shatters the fragile remains of my self-control. I can't take it anymore.

Throwing my arms around his neck, I pull his face down until my lips are pressed against his.

# CHAPTER 11

## LUKA

*S*he kissed me. The feel of Harper's soft lips moving against mine stole the air from my lungs, leaving me frozen in place. My only regret is that I failed to match the movement of her sweet mouth before she pulled away. Her dark-blue eyes widened as soon as she opened them. She let out a kind of nervous squeak, apologized once more, then grabbed the carrier and Viper's food, and ran inside. Her reaction was adorable, but I do not like the way it left things between us.

It all happened so quickly; I did not get the chance to tell her that the single greatest moment of my existence required no apology. I did not get the chance to assure my mate that her embrace and the feel of her breasts pressed against my stomach are not unwelcome. Not in the least. And that there is so much more I wish to do.

I want to hold her firmly against me, to run my nose along the length of her throat, so I can inhale huge lungfuls of her scent instead of sneaking a whiff here and there when I think she will not notice. Then, I would taste her skin, her smooth, creamy flesh, as I cup her breast, the weight of it filling my palm as I rub her nipple into a stiff peak beneath her shirt.

Sighing wistfully at the ways I would make her moan in my arms has me adjusting the front of my pants, which feel uncomfortably tight at the moment. Being anywhere near Harper makes me hard, but this is another level of discomfort.

My draxilio does not stop growling on my walk home. He is deeply disappointed I did not break down Harper's front door and claim her body.

When I arrive at the apartment, I do not stop to greet my brothers where they sit on the couch watching another show called *Golden Girls*. Instead, I rush into the bathroom attached to my bedroom, turn on the water in the shower, shove my pants to my knees, and stroke my cock as I imagine what would have happened between Harper and me if she had let me into her home.

Picturing her slowly peeling her clothes off and the dips and curves of her body bared for my eyes has me spilling my seed into my palm. I envision the tips of my fingers digging into the soft skin of her stomach and hips as she rolls her body against me, her heavy breasts bouncing with the movement. I release twice more before my body feels relaxed enough to sleep. And even in sleep, all I see is her.

The next morning, I meet Harper at her home to walk her to work. She seems just as nervous as she was last night, which bothers me. She apologizes once more for the kiss, but before I can tell her she does not need to, she asks me how much my bodyguard services will cost. It deflates the hope blooming in my chest that I was finally making progress with my mate. For whatever reason, she acts as if she would like to forget the kiss.

"I do not require compensation for keeping you safe," I tell her. My tone is cold, but that is how my heart feels, so there is no point in hiding it.

When she insists on paying me, I bark out, "No, you will not. That is the end of the matter."

Minutes pass as we walk in a loaded silence. Eventually, Harper starts talking about the appointments on her schedule for the day, and what she will need to do for each patient. Her words are rushed, and her voice is a pitch higher than usual.

"Ugh, and my mom called this morning, asking if I was planning on going to mass on Sunday," she says. "I love her, but I haven't been to Sunday mass in years. I'm not sure why she keeps asking other than to make me feel guilty for skipping it."

"Are you close with your parents?"

"Not like my brother is," she mutters quietly. "She also reminded me about the play my nephew is in next Saturday. That, I definitely can't skip."

I love hearing about her family, and the many tasks that fill her days. She could go into a detailed explanation of the history of cement, and I would hang on her every word.

"Tell me about your brother."

She groans. "He's...fine. My parents hoped he would grow up to be a doctor, which he did. Graduated somewhere in the middle of his class, whereas I was my vet school's valedictorian, but whatever."

"They do not acknowledge your accomplishments compared to his?"

Harper shakes her head. "No, not in the same way." She stops to face me. "I know they're proud of me, but they act like my brother is a hero for having an MD and my DVM is just a cute little piece of paper that represents a hobby and not a career I've worked my ass off for."

"That must be frustrating," I tell her. I do not like seeing her mouth forming a frown. Such beautiful lips are not meant to take that shape.

"It really is," she agrees.

"You care for creatures who struggle to survive in this world. Many of whom, without your intervention, would not make it."

Her frown fades, giving way to a smile that makes my heart stop. "Thank you for saying that."

"Did Viper serve as an adequate bodyguard during the night?"

Harper chuckles. "He did. I think he hissed whenever he heard the wind, so he's willing to protect me even from nature." She shoots me an odd glance, and then asks, "You don't like hunting, do you?"

"Hunting?"

"Yeah," she says with a nod. "Trekking out into the woods with a gun and killing defenseless animals."

"You mean for food?" I ask. "I suppose I–"

"Well, no," she interjects. "Not hunting for survival. That's different. Would you hunt an animal just to kill it and display part of its body as a trophy?"

If she is trying to maintain a neutral tone, she is failing. It is clear hunting is not something she has any interest in. But apart from that, the concept seems silly to me. "Death by a gunshot is an easy death. The animal would have no chance of surviving. How could that be considered a victory worthy of a trophy?"

Harper's expression turns warm. She is pleased. "Agreed."

Then she starts telling me about her superior, Dr. Brooks, and how he repeatedly refuses to nurture Ryan's desire to learn more as the head technician. "It's almost like, if Ryan can't afford to pay vet school tuition, he doesn't deserve to learn anything new. What the fuck kind of attitude is that? Why does he feel the need to gate-keep certain information? Ryan is brilliant, and his brain is a sponge. He's eager to learn everything he can, and *that's* the kind of employee every clinic needs."

Though she speaks fondly of another human male, I do not feel even a flicker of jealousy when she defends him so passionately. She seems protective of him in the same way I am protective of my brothers.

"You know what?" she says as she continues walking. "Fuck it. I'm not even going to ask for Dr. Brooks's permission to teach him surgical techniques or how to extract a rotten tooth during a dental cleaning. I'll just show him after hours. Dr. Brooks will never know."

When we reach the clinic, I ask about Colin. "Has he continued his attempts to contact you?"

"Not since I ignored his invitation to meet him for a second date. I think he got the hint," she says, relief thick in her voice.

"Good," I tell her. "I shall meet you here at the same time?"

She nods, and I wait until she's inside before walking away.

\* \* \*

I fear I am missing something. Colin continues to evade me, and I do not understand how. After leaving the clinic, I asked Jay to assist me in finding Colin's place of work, which he did quite easily.

"Colin White, here he is," Jay said. "He works at Revere Creek Capital." It was listed on Colin's book-faces page as his employer, but when I spoke to the tall woman at the big desk in the lobby of their building, she said she had never heard of a Colin White. It does not make sense.

Immediately after, I flew over the place I assume is his home, but his scent was too stale for me to bother knocking on the door. He was not there either. Where is he? How could he continue hiding from me?

Though, I suppose it is enough to remain by Harper's side. Colin will not get anywhere near my mate as long I am with her.

Knocking on the back door three times, I wait for Harper to let me into the clinic. She greets me with a bright smile as she zips up her long wool coat. Its pink shade matches her lips as they close around an orange straw that disappears into a large cup of ice and pale brown liquid.

"Interesting beverage choice on this frigid day," I note.

She looks down, then purses her lips as she meets my gaze. "It's iced coffee. Iced coffee is a year-round delicacy." Her tone is serious, but in a playful way, as if I should know this already. "Eliza got it for me this afternoon since I had to work through lunch."

My draxilio bristles with unease.

"You are hungry?" I ask, searching my mind for a place to feed my mate.

"Always," she replies, taking another sip of her icy drink.

As I consider where I can take her for a meal, my phone vibrates against my thigh.

> Jay: Talia's last night at TB. She's finishing up in 10 and bringing a feast over to your place. Get ready to eat your body weight in Crunchwrap Supremes.

I turn to Harper. "Would you like to come to my home for dinner? I will still escort you back to your home after, of course."

Her eyes swirl with affection as she places her hand on my arm. "I'd love that."

Instead of walking, Harper calls a cab to take us to my apartment. Her leg is sore today, and though I offered to carry her, she seemed to prefer this method of transportation.

"This is it," I tell her as we exit the elevator.

Talia, Jay, and my brothers are all huddled around the kitchen island when we enter, pulling various tacos, burritos, and packets of fire sauce out of plastic bags. They greet us with smiles and cheers.

Harper smiles warmly at everyone, but I can see the uncertainty in her eyes. She is nervous.

"These are my dear friends, Talia and Jay," I say to Harper. "Jay is the first person we met here in Boston, and he has shown us incredible kindness. Talia is Jay's girlfriend and is celebrating the end of her time as a Taco Bell employee."

"Hey, Harper," Jay calls, waving a burrito in his hand.

"Hi, Harper," Talia says, coming over to shake my mate's hand. "Nice to finally meet you."

"Ditto," Harper says, "and congrats on this new chapter you're about to begin."

"Thanks," Talia replies. "Jay and I are really excited. We've been saving up for years so we can move to Colorado and open a bakery. And whenever weed gets legalized, we'll serve edibles too."

"Oh, how exciting."

"These are my brothers," I interject, gesturing in their direction. They drop the food from their hands and form a line in front of Harper, eager for the introduction. "Mylo, Kyan, and Zev, and, of course, Axil you have met."

They are polite and warm to my mate as they greet her, as expected. When Axil releases Harper's hand, he stares at her cane. I am about to admonish him for it, but he asks, "Do you find your cane provides the support you need, Harper?"

She sneaks a surprised glance at me before answering, "Um, I guess? It's fine."

"Hmm," Axil mutters, scratching at his beard. "May I see it?"

Harper shrugs and hands it to him.

He thoughtfully inspects the curved handgrip, the shaft, and the tip before handing it back. "I have become interested in woodworking recently. A cane would be a welcome challenge. Might I have the opportunity to make you one?"

"Sure," Harper says to Axil. "If it's not too much trouble, of course."

"Woodworking? When did that become an interest of yours?" I ask, tilting my head to the side.

"You have not been home much lately, brother," he replies with a smirk. "I have developed many interests."

I suppose he is right. I have not spent enough time with my brothers lately, having been consumed with thoughts of Harper and whether she is safe.

"Don't be shy, you two," Talia calls out. "We've got a year's worth of tacos over here."

I assist Harper with filling her plate, then fill my own before I stand at the counter across from her. She shoots me a shy smile, and I realize how at peace I feel at this moment with my mate and brothers in the same place.

"Luka, I hope this isn't a date or anything," Talia says from across the kitchen island. "Because bringing a girl back to your apartment to eat Taco Bell with your brothers? Yikes."

"No, this is not a date," I say in a rush, at the same time Harper says, "I actually like Taco Bell."

Her face falls when she registers what I said, and I am puzzled. Surely, she knows if this were a date, I would take her somewhere other than my apartment, yes? Somewhere better. Nicer. Perhaps the fancy pizza place with the strange name. Papa Gino's, I think it is called. Talia and Jay speak of it as if it is the epitome of fancy dining.

"Talia, did you ever speak to your boss about my salad recipe?" Mylo asks in an obvious attempt to break the tension.

"Mylo, honey," Talia begins, patting the back of Mylo's hand in a placating way. "Apple slices, fries, and iceberg lettuce with fire sauce on top is not a salad."

"It is though. It has lettuce," he replies, looking around at our brothers for support.

"I do not like it with apples," Kyan notes. "Just eat the fries, lettuce, and sauce."

"But the apples add a sweet element to the entire dish." Mylo's gaze lands on Harper. "Harper, please explain it to them."

Harper's mouth falls open as she struggles to select her next words.

Talia interjects. "Not sure if you know this, but they escaped a cult not long ago," she tells Harper. "Hence..." she waves her hand in front of Mylo, "this whole thing."

"I heard," Harper replies in an empathetic tone. Then her eyes meet mine, and I swallow as they begin to swirl with heat. "I really appreciate their bluntness though. And how they don't seem to care what anyone thinks. It's refreshing."

After we eat, Harper and I take a cab back to her house. I take her hand to help her out of the cab, and she does not let go, even when she is on her feet. Her hand is tiny compared to mine, and it reminds me that I was made to protect her, even if the only protection I can provide in this moment is warmth against the cold. She pulls me along to her front door, and as she takes her keys out of her bag, she tilts her face up to look at me. "Wanna come inside for a drink?"

I am not thirsty, but if she keeps looking at me like that, my throat will turn into an arid desert in no time. "Yes," I rasp, "I would like that very much."

She locks the door behind us, and as soon as she removes her coat, her hands are on me. Her breath catches and her eyes are swirling with carnal heat. My cock pulses as her fingers wrap around the collar of my jacket and she pulls my face down until it hovers just above hers. "I don't have anything to drink. It was a lie to get you in here. I'm sorry."

"Stop. Apologizing," I growl as I cradle the back of her head and pull her closer.

When our lips touch this time, I am anything but frozen. This time,

I take her mouth with the desperate hunger that surges within me. She parts her lips for me immediately, welcoming me in for a taste. Gods, the taste of her is so sweet, it almost snaps me in half. I twist a hand in her hair, and the other sinks into the soft flesh of her hip, holding her in place. I could stay here for eternity, I realize, drinking her in and running my hands along her glorious body.

The steady purr from my draxilio does not surprise me at all. He is pleased with this new development.

My body shakes with need as I back my mate against the nearest wall, her hips rolling against me. I need more, but memories of the first night we met flood my mind and I worry I will do the wrong thing and upset her. How do I approach this without scaring her away with the wrong words?

Ducking my head, I kiss along Harper's neck as I stroke up and down her arms. It seems a safe spot to touch, so I continue as her moans fill the room. The blunt tips of her tiny fingers dig into my back as she arches against me, and my cock hardens, practically reaching for her as it presses against my pants.

Then she lets out a frustrated groan and pushes my palm against her breast. "Fucking touch me already, Luka."

I pull back to look at her, needing clarification before I proceed. "Anywhere?"

She kisses me again, hard and deep, then says, "Anywhere," just before the soft tip of her tongue traces my bottom lip.

The list of ways in which I long to touch Harper is endless, and I hoped someday she would let me explore her body properly, but tonight, I have one very specific idea of how to bring her pleasure.

My hand drifts down her rounded tummy and beneath the loose waistband of her work pants. Her breath turns ragged when I run a finger down her slit, still covered with the puzzling scrap of fabric called *underwear* that humans prefer. Her stance widens and her cane clatters to the floor as she pushes against my hand, adding pressure as she grinds against me.

"Yes," she says in a panting hiss. The sight of her eyes pinched shut in ecstasy is one I will never forget.

My fingers deftly move her underwear aside, and a deep, rumbling groan rips from my throat the second I am met with her soaked folds. I pay close attention to every sharp intake of breath, every moan, and the way her hips buck against me as I run my fingers back and forth over her clit, trying to determine what she most prefers.

When I insert two fingers into her body and run the pad of my thumb over her clit, she quakes in my arms.

"Tell me what you want," I growl into the crook of her neck before lightly nipping at the skin over her racing pulse. "I will give you everything."

She gasps and pushes my fingers deeper into her core. "Just don't stop. Don't ever stop."

Harper comes undone seconds later, gripping my shoulders tightly while she rides out her release. I am certain there are marks on my skin. The thought fills my chest with pride. I want her marks all over my body.

My phone vibrates in my back pocket, and I ignore it as I capture her mouth once more. She makes needy, eager sounds against my mouth as I reach for the bottom hem of her work shirt. But when my phone vibrates a second time, I wonder if this is a call I should ignore.

Growling, I break away from my mate and flip open my phone with a bark. "What!"

"It is Zev. We require your assistance, brother."

"Zev?" I shout, "What has happened?"

Zev lowers his voice to a whisper. "Kyan wanted to see if he had your same power of influence. We located a group of finance bros at the dance hall and his attempt was unsuccessful. There was a fight. We won, of course, but the police put us in handcuffs and now we are in jail."

"You what?" I yell, my anger reaching a level it has not in a long time. Not only did my brothers interrupt me while I was pleasuring my mate, but now they are in trouble with the local authorities. I run a hand through my hair, tugging on the strands as Zev gives me directions to where I need to go. "I shall be there shortly," I say before hanging up.

"What's going on?" Harper asks, her lips swollen from my kisses and her hair a wild mess around her head. There has never been a creature more radiant than her. I am certain of it.

"My brothers got into a fight. I must bail them out of jail."

"Oh my god. That's crazy," she says with a hand covering her mouth. "I can't even picture your brothers getting angry, to be honest."

*You have never seen them whipping through the sky, trying to set each other's tails on fire,* I want to tell her. I do not though, because that is not information she currently needs. "They are sometimes wild beasts," I eventually say.

Giving her a final kiss that I hope will leave her thinking of me until the morning, I bid her farewell and make my way toward the police station. It is a miserable walk, as I am still painfully hard, which makes me even angrier at my brothers. How dare they disrupt me when I am pleasuring my mate?

I explain who I am to the short male with pale, freckled skin at the front desk. He leads me down a narrow hallway to an area with *holding cells* as is indicated on the white-lettered sign, and I am introduced to the policeman who received the disturbance call. He tells me the same as Zev did, minus the first bit about Kyan attempting to use my powers.

Though I am reluctant to help my brothers out of this mess, as it was so easily avoidable in the first place, I focus on the policeman's pulse and the feel of his mind as I pull him into my clutches. I explain that he is mistaken, that no fight occurred at the dance hall, and that the entire ordeal was nothing more than a miscommunication between a few drunken fellows.

He nods robotically, agreeing with the points I make as he lets my brothers out of their cage.

I do not speak to any of them on our walk home. My mind races with the ways this night could have gone so much worse. They could have killed the humans they sparred with. Then what? We would all be exposed for what we are and any chance we have of finding our mates and living a life of happiness would vanish.

"You did not know of your power until we arrived on Earth, brother," Kyan says once we enter our apartment. "We all might have the same power, and we cannot be certain of that unless we test it."

"That is a good point," I begin, "but when you realized you did not have my power, you tried to steal his wallet anyway. How do you explain that?"

Kyan says nothing. Eventually, he shrugs. "I was upset that I did not have your gift."

"Even now, you do not see the danger you put us in," I mutter as I lean my forearms on the kitchen island.

"That male deserved the swollen eye we gave him," Mylo says with a scoff as he plops down on the couch.

"I left my mate to rescue you fools," I shout, tired of being the only one who walks this Earth with the right amount of caution. There is nothing more I wish to say to them, so I throw up my hands and stomp down the hall to my bedroom. As I reach for the door handle, Axil calls my name.

He looks embarrassed and remorseful, as he should.

"I am deeply sorry we ruined your evening," he says, scratching the back of his neck. "It got out of hand so quickly. But it should not have occurred at all, and for that, I apologize."

"Why did he even bother trying to steal a wallet? We have amassed enough funds from the finance bros thus far to keep us clothed and fed. There was no need for what took place tonight."

"No, there was not," he agrees. "We are bored. All of us. We remain here all day, every day, watching the TV. The only places we are allowed to go without you are to Jay's pawn shop and Taco Bell."

It is true that I have ordered them to remain here, but it is for their own good. When I am not present, they get into trouble, as they did tonight. "How can you expect me to trust you enough to dismiss that order? Look at what occurred this night."

Axil's gaze drops to the floor. I do not need to command him to dip his snout. He knows the magnitude of this mistake.

"I cannot do this for the rest of my days, Axil," I tell him with a sigh. "I cannot use my powers to clean up the messes you leave behind. I refuse."

"I understand. It will not happen again."

I go to bed worried that it will happen again, and that next time, I will not be able to undo it. The only sliver of solace I get is the rich, heady flavor of Harper's essence still on my fingers, which I lick clean until I can taste her no more.

# CHAPTER 12

## HARPER

*D*ays pass as Luka and I settle into a routine. He shows up at my place with a medium, French vanilla iced coffee with extra cream and extra sugar, which is my drink of choice from Dunkin' Donuts, and today is no exception.

I squeal at the sight of it this morning. Sleep has been hard to come by since the night he had me pinned against the wall and rocked my world. I haven't been able to stop thinking about it and wondering when it'll happen again.

Each night, I invite him inside after he walks me home, and he comes in, but it's just to have a quick visit with Viper and to make sure the place is secure. Then he gives me an excuse as to why he can't stay, always having to do with his brothers, and leaves.

I know he was really upset after bailing them out of jail, but they're grown men, for Christ's sake. Can't they take care of themselves? Does he really need to babysit them every single night?

It makes me wonder if he's telling the truth. Because if he is still into me, why hasn't he kissed me again? He kisses me on the cheek as he says goodbye, but shit, my mom does that too. And his kiss was good. It wasn't some sloppy, middle school tongue slap session. It was *hot.* So hot, it curled my damn toes. The evidence that he enjoyed it pushed against my stomach the whole time, so I know he was into it too.

When we reach the back door of the clinic, he leans down and presses a chaste kiss to my cheek, and says, "Same time? Three knocks?"

"Yep," I reply, in an exasperated tone I can't hide. "See you then."

The day passes too slowly for my liking, giving me plenty of chances to overthink things with Luka. That night at my place, I had to yell at him to grope me. Does he need that kind of signal every time?

Luka seems confident enough to make the first move on his own. He's not some shy teenage boy.

No, no, it can't be that he's too shy. That doesn't make sense.

My phone buzzes on my desk, causing me to jump. Excitement twists my stomach at the thought of it being Luka, but when I look at the screen, my excitement evaporates.

"Hi, Mom."

"Honey, we missed you at mass on Sunday," she chides me.

"Oh, yeah. I'm sorry, I had a tricky case with a patient I got caught up in," I lie.

"Derek and Faith came, of course," she says of my brother and sister-in-law. "They come every week, even with how busy Derek is with his practice."

I'm so not in the mood for this right now. "Yeah, it's a wonder he even has time to take a piss when he's up to his elbows in all those stuffed noses, wax-filled ears, and sore throats."

"Harper Marie, that is out of line. Your brother works hard."

I want so badly to point out the ten weeks of vacation time he took last year, but I don't. It would be petty, and it would upset my mom even more than she is now, which I truly had no intention of doing. "I'm sorry, Mom. I'm just having a tough day."

"It's okay, sweetie. We'll see you on Saturday for Nathan's play, right? He's the star, you know."

Right. My nephew's play. "Yes, I'll be there."

"Having grandchildren is such a blessing. I only hope someday you'll get to experience the same divine joy."

"Okay, see you later, Mom. Bye."

It's impressive how quickly she can make me so angry I want to scream, then bury me under a pile of guilt to the point where I apologize to her, and then bring me right back to the brink of having a rage stroke. If it weren't the main cause of my many gray hairs, I'd compliment her on it.

The afternoon is busier than the morning, which I'm grateful for. It's easy to forget about guy drama when there's a sick puppy in front of you.

I flip open my phone to text Luka that my appointments are wrapped for the day and I'm way too tired to stay late tonight when a familiar voice in the lobby sends goose bumps across my skin.

"Um, she's not here," I hear Eliza stammer when Colin asks if I can examine his dog quickly.

"There's no doctor here that can look at my dog? She's been puking for two days."

Eliza pauses, then replies, "Let me see if we can get you in."

She meets me in the hallway with panicked eyes. "What the fuck?" she mouths silently. She pulls me into my office and asks what we should do.

I hate that there's only one answer. It doesn't matter what he's done, I'm not about to let his dog suffer. I can't.

"Put him in room two," I tell her. She bites her lip, looking as if she wants to stall until we come up with something else. But there is nothing else. If we send him away, I'm always going to wonder about that dog. "It's fine," I reassure her. "I'll text Luka right now to meet me here."

That seems to comfort her enough. "Okay, fine, but Ryan and I will be listening through the door. If he tries to pull anything," she picks up the tiny stapler from my desk, "I'm putting about seven of these in his forehead."

I chuckle as she goes back to the lobby and escorts Colin into the exam room. Pulling out my phone, I send Luka a text:

He's here. Help.

Then I take a deep breath and enter the room. "Hi, Colin. What seems to be going on with Gidget?" I ask, focusing on the medical chart in my hands.

"Harper, it's good to see you."

He's smiling at me. I feel it. He hasn't even put his dog on the exam table yet.

"Uh-huh. Looks like Gidget has been vomiting for two days. Can you describe the color and consistency of the vomit?"

"I've been worried about you ever since you were a no-show for our date."

He can't be serious.

"I never agreed to go on that date. You sent flowers and told me where to meet you. That's not a request for a date, that's a demand. After what happened, you can't exp–"

"I said I was sorry about that," he interrupts. "It was a regrettable moment, but not a reflection of the kind of guy I am. I swear."

As if his promises hold any weight.

"Can you put her on the table for me?" I ask, trying to shift the conversation to the sick two-year-old Bichon Frisé.

To my surprise and delight, he does. Pulling out my stethoscope, I listen to Gidget's heart and lungs, both of which sound normal.

"The vomit, what was the color and consistency?" I ask again. "And has she eaten anything since this started?"

"Um, clear. Watery," he mutters dismissively. "Why didn't you show up for our date, Harper? I waited for you for two hours."

*Focus on Gidget. Focus on Gidget.*

"Her pupils are slightly dilated, but her gums look healthy, so that's a good sign," I tell him, ignoring his ridiculous question. "Has she eaten anything in the last twenty-four hours?"

He wraps his fingers around my wrist and squeezes to the point of pain, holding me in place. "Do you have any idea how bad you made me look? Making me wait for you like that?"

"Let go," I say, my voice shaking as I attempt to pull away.

Gidget lets out a whimper of distress as I continue trying to yank my arm free.

The door to the exam room flings open so hard, the top hinge breaks off, skittering across the linoleum floor. Luka fills the door frame; he even has to duck slightly as he enters. Eliza and Ryan stand on either side of him, and all three of them hold Colin in a murderous gaze.

"It's okay, Luka," I tell him, mostly to keep him from scaring Gidget. The poor thing keeps whimpering, and none of this is her fault.

"It is not okay," Luka snarls, his teeth gritted as he stalks slowly toward Colin.

Colin backs against the wall, his hands raised. "Nothing happened, man. We were just talking. She overreacted, that's all."

Ryan sidesteps the group and lifts Gidget off the exam table and puts her on the floor, her leash in hand.

"You put your hands on her again, Colin?" Luka asks, stepping into Colin's space, forcing him backward, until he bumps his head against the wall.

"You will leave now," Luka tells him. "Take your business else-where, and if you ever contact Harper again, I want you to understand that I will turn every bone inside your body to dust, and I will do so with a smile."

Colin doesn't reply. He just cowers until Luka lets him pass, then he grabs Gidget's leash from Ryan and storms out the front door.

And because I can't help myself, I yell after him, "Don't feed her anything for twenty-four hours, and if the vomiting stops, give her small amounts of boiled chicken and white rice until she feels better."

Eliza tugs on my arm to pull me back inside, then locks the front door. "Seriously?" she asks with an incredulous look.

"I'm not going to let Gidget suffer just because her owner is an entitled jackass."

Ryan shakes his head at me, but not without a smile.

Luka still looks like he wants to kill Colin. To ease the tension, I wrap my arms around his middle until I feel his arms settle against my back. "Thank you for coming."

"Did you think I would not?"

"No, I knew you would, and I'm grateful you did."

He pulls back and crooks a finger under my chin, lifting it until our eyes meet. "I will not fail you."

Luka and I pile into Ryan's backseat while he and Eliza sit in the front, and Ryan drives us to my place. It's a very tight squeeze, having Luka in the back of a Jetta, but the fact that he can barely fit in a normal-sized car makes me even more attracted to him. He needs a car built for giants.

Not only am I sore, but I'm frazzled and shaky after seeing Colin, so there is no way I was going to walk home. When we arrive, I thank Ryan and Eliza for their support and pull Luka inside before he can protest.

"I shall check on Viper and make sure everything is secure," he says as he removes his coat and hangs it on the hook by the door.

I let him go, knowing he won't be comfortable until he knows that Colin isn't hiding behind a curtain in my bedroom. Quietly, I climb the stairs to my bedroom and stifle a laugh as I hear Viper hiss and hop off the bed. He scampers past me with a high-pitched mew. Luka has just finished checking my closet when I step inside the room, closing the door behind me and leaning against it.

"Are you well?" he asks, his eyes wide with concern as he steps in front of me.

"I'm well, yes."

His fingers brush against my cheek, and I close my eyes as I lean into his touch.

"You are still frightened," he says as more of a statement than a question. Though I suppose it's not a difficult assumption to make after what happened.

"A little," I tell him. "But I think," I pause, searching for the words. I'm trying to be seductive, but that doesn't come naturally to me. Instead, my fear entwines with the confusion I've felt from trying to read Luka's mixed signals, causing me to snap. "Why haven't you kissed me?"

"Why have I not kissed you?" he repeats in a slower, more menacing tone as he places his palms on either side of my head, caging me in.

His focused attention makes me squirm. "I-I had a good time when we," I stammer, "when I...when you had me—"

"When I had you pinned against the wall, and you fucked my hand?"

I've never heard him curse before. It sends a shiver down my spine.

He leans down and runs his nose along my neck, breathing me in. "I have not kissed you, Harper, because the next time I do, I will not be able to stop." His voice turns rough with need. "Once I taste you here," he runs the rough pad of his thumb along my lower lip, "I will need to taste you here." He drops his hand between my legs and traces my slit, causing me to suck in a breath. "And after I run my hands and tongue all over your body, I will sink into your sweet cunt and make you come over and over," he nips at the spot where my neck and shoulder meet, "until you beg me to stop."

Then, suddenly, he pushes himself off the door and backs away, leaving me panting. "I do not know if that is something you want."

"You should've asked," I spit out, taking a step toward him.

His surprised expression boggles me. How clear must I make it that I want him?

He closes the distance between us and cradles my head in his hand. "You are certain?"

"Yes."

It comes out as a desperate plea in the form of a whisper, but before I can feel self-conscious about my obvious desire for him, he claims my lips in a hard, searing kiss.

I let out a squeak against his mouth as he lifts me, but he pulls back just far enough to say, "I have you," and my worries vanish. His long fingers grip and massage my ass as he carries me to the bed, dropping me softly onto my back.

He unties the laces of my sneakers, pressing a kiss to each ankle as he removes my shoes and socks. Then he kisses the tip of each toe while stroking his thumb along the arches of my feet.

"Oh my god," I moan when he shifts his focus to my heel.

I hear him chuckle quietly. "Feels good?"

"Mmm," is all I can manage. That's how good it feels.

Luka gets to his feet and peels my pants off slowly. My shirt follows. Then my sports bra. When I'm topless in front of him, his heavy-lidded gaze feels so intense that I move to cover my chest with my hands.

"No," he commands, grabbing my wrists and holding them still. "Do not hide from me."

I drop my arms to my sides as he hooks his fingers around the sides of my unsexy, high-waisted beige underwear and pulls them down my legs. He stares at my bush, and again, it's hard not to feel self-conscious.

I would've shaved had I known I'd be getting naked with Luka today. I start to tell him that, but before I can, he shoves his nose into my curls and inhales deeply. Instead of an exhalation, Luka growls as he opens his eyes, and I've never felt more wanted by anyone in my entire life.

"Your scent," he says, his voice so low, I barely recognize it. "It is so much stronger here."

"Okay," I whisper, not knowing what to say. "That's a good thing?"

Luka doesn't answer with words. He parts my folds and shoves his tongue between them, lapping at my core as if it's a melting ice cream cone. We let out matching moans that fill the room. My hips buck against his face as a layer of goosebumps races across my skin. "Yes, like that," I cry out as he replaces his tongue with two fingers pumping in and out as he strokes the tip of his tongue against the side of my clit. "Just like that."

When he sucks on the swollen bud, I lose myself completely. My body seizes as my orgasm hits me, wave after wave of blinding pleasure. I hear the rustle of clothes hitting the floor before Luka covers me with his body and wraps me in his arms. He presses gentle kisses all over my forehead and eyes, and when I start to come down, I feel the large head of his cock pressing against my entrance.

"Are you ready, my mate?" he asks, his gray eyes shining with desire and adoration. His wording is a bit strange, but it's hard to focus on that when the steel rod between his legs continues brushing against my clit.

I nod, spreading wider for him. Before I have the chance to look, he pushes into me slowly, filling me. With every inch, I find it harder to breathe.

"Relax, *ledai*, you can take me. All of me," he whispers against my mouth before pressing a deep, bruising kiss to my lips.

Pinching my eyes closed, I focus on the kiss as I envision my body opening for him. My muscles relax, and I press my hands into his lower back, demanding more. He breaks the kiss to look at me.

Brushing my nose against his, I kiss him again, and in a panting whisper I say, "More."

In one motion, he sinks all the way in until our hips meet. I let out a silent scream as he pulls out almost completely, then drives into me again. I'm stuffed, stretched wider than I ever thought possible, and I haven't even gotten a glimpse of his massive dick yet.

He picks up the pace, and my nails bite into his back as I hold on for the ride. Stars explode behind my eyelids seconds later, and I pull him with me into the darkness of sated bliss. He roars as he comes, his hot seed filling my channel. We fall asleep wrapped around each other, his cock still hard inside me, until we wake in the middle of the night for another round, this time with my feet in the air as he pounds into me while standing at the foot of the bed.

Luka makes me come three more times before the sun rises, and I smile at the parts of my body that are sore when the light streams through my window. When I roll over to face him, I find his side of the bed empty.

There's no note, and the sheets are cold, as if he's been gone for hours.

# CHAPTER 13

## LUKA

$\mathcal{M}$y steps are light, and my smile is wide as I make my way back to Harper's home from the café two blocks down. I know she enjoys bagels, so I bought one of each kind for her breakfast. She can choose which one she likes best.

A tingling sensation still fills me at the memory of her cunt gripping me, milking me as I emptied my seed into her warm, welcoming body. It was the best moment of my existence, and that continues to happen with Harper—a new experience claiming the top spot among my memories. I wonder if it will always be this way with her, with each day turning out better than the last.

One problem remains: my inability to sleep next to my mate. There is nothing I want more than to listen to her deep, even breaths as she sleeps soundly in my arms, but if I were to fall asleep beside her and she were to wake before me, she would discover me in my true state. In sleep, I cannot mask my blue skin and horns. It is an ability that requires little focus but steady consciousness. She still does not know what I am. How would she react if she found out?

I will tell her. I must. If she is to become my mate, this is not a secret I can continue to keep. The closer I get to her, the harder it is to hide the truth. I am not yet certain she would accept me in my true state. Until I am confident, I will not scare her. More importantly, so she will not inform the local authorities of us, I must keep this part of myself hidden.

Closing the front door quietly behind me, I am met with the aggressive hiss of Viper sitting on the front window ledge, eyeing me with pure hatred.

Pulling my lips back, I snarl at him. Viper's tail swishes back and forth as we continue to stare at each other before he eventually leaps down with a clipped mew and races up the stairs.

"You're back," Harper says from the top of the stairs.

"With food," I reply, lifting my arms to show her the containers of hot coffee and the bag of bagels in my hand.

A smile tugs at her lips, and I briefly forget how to breathe. "Oh!" she exclaims in a much happier tone as she comes down the stairs. "I thought you went back to your apartment," she mutters quietly before taking a sip of her coffee.

"Without saying goodbye to you?" I ask incredulously. Does she truly think so little of me? "I would never do that, Harper."

She rubs her hand across her forehead. "Ugh, I'm sorry. You didn't leave a note, so I assumed the worst."

I take the coffee from her hands and place it on the short table in front of her couch. She comes willingly into my arms and sighs when her head rests against my chest. "I should have left a note. This is my fault, not yours."

She looks up at me, and I count the subtle flecks of gold near the pupils of her big blue eyes. There are six. "What did I tell you about apologizing?"

Harper chuckles, the sound so light and melodic that longing to hear it for the rest of my days strikes me deep in the gut.

We sit next to each other on the couch, and I eat the three bagels she does not want as she tells me about her nephew's play the following night. I was planning to escort her to and from the play already, but when she invites me to stay and watch the play by her side, I am caught off guard in the best possible way.

"I would love to come," I tell her. "Will I meet your parents then?"

"Yep," she says with a roll of her eyes. "The whole family will be there."

"They are happy together? Your parents."

Her face softens as she considers my question. "Yeah, I think so. I mean, I don't know what they have in common, other than Catholicism, of course." She lets out a playful laugh. "My dad was born in Ireland and came here with his parents when he was sixteen. My mom was one of the first people he met here. I think she helped him get acclimated. He was really shy. Still is, in fact. They met at church, and it has sort of been their thing ever since."

I let her words settle in my mind as I picture a young male in a new place and a kind, warm-hearted female making him feel less alone. No matter where such a meeting occurs, it is not difficult to see how that would evolve into long-lasting love.

"I am looking forward to this play," I tell her honestly.

"And if Colin shows up," she says with a shaky breath, "he probably won't, but if he does…"

"I shall end him before he gets anywhere near you or your family."

She laughs as if my words were a joke. When Harper sees the seriousness in my expression, she tilts her head to the side and asks, "You'd really do that for me?"

"There is nothing I would not do for you."

# CHAPTER 14

## HARPER

"*I* think I need a breather," I tell Luka through panting breaths as I roll onto my back. A sheen of sweat covers my skin from the second orgasm he's given me since walking me home from work tonight, and my stomach growls loudly.

"You are hungry," he says, immediately pulling himself out of bed. "Let us fix that."

I bite my lip as I watch him bend to grab his mesh shorts off the floor, giving me a spectacular view of his tight, coin-deflecting ass. I can't help but frown the moment he's covered up.

"Come, *ledai*," he says, holding out a hand. "Let me feed you." Placing my palm in his, he pulls me to my feet and hands me my cane. Then he retrieves his dark-purple T-shirt off the edge of the dresser and gently pulls it over my head, straightening it and my hair before pressing his forehead against mine. "You glow like the sun."

"You lie," I say with a smile before planting a smacking kiss on his lips.

We order pizza and a few sides, and I show him what an actual salad tastes like without the apple slices, french fries, and fire sauce. He seems to like it, but not as much as the strange mix Mylo makes at home. Who can blame him? Any salad with fries will always beat a salad without.

When we finish eating, we climb back into bed and I put on a movie, *Fever Pitch*, before snuggling into his arms. He listens intently as I describe how it felt to watch the 2004 Red Sox win the world series. "Don't get me wrong, this year's win was thrilling too, but 2004 was special. It took them eighty-six years to win that trophy. I'll never forget it."

After the movie, I suggest we put on some old episodes of *Lost*, just to see if he likes it. I try summarizing it for him to really sell it, but his brow furrows with confusion the deeper I go into the story, so I tell him it'll all make sense once he starts watching, which isn't exactly true, since it's *Lost*, but he's a good sport and seems eager to indulge me.

A few minutes into the pilot, Luka is already leaning forward and barely blinking, his attention locked on the screen. He's hooked, and it makes me ten times more attracted to him than I already was.

"Why were they brought to the island?" he asks at one point.

"That hasn't been explained yet," I tell him. "It's one of the big questions that keeps coming up."

Hours pass and Luka shows no interest in taking a break. I fall asleep halfway through the episode about Locke's backstory, and later I wake to the credits rolling on the TV and Luka's lips leaving a hot trail along my left hip. "Mmm," I moan, shoving my fingers through his hair.

His hands replace his lips, and he begins massaging the area, going deeper into my tender flesh as he gauges my reaction. "Does that feel good?"

"It really does," I tell him. "Move down just a little though?" He does, and my breath whooshes out of me when his thumb strokes across the spot I apply ice to several times a week. I used to go for a weekly massage after my accident, but since the divorce, it's a luxury I can't afford, at least, not that frequently. None of those massages were like this, though. This is Luka, and there is deep tenderness in every one of his touches.

He focuses on my hip for several minutes, then moves down my thigh, pausing when he reaches my scar. It stretches from an inch above my knee to two inches below, and the surrounding skin is discolored, uneven, and bumpy. Blood rushes to my cheeks as I drop my hand to cover the area, but Luka quickly bats it away before lowering his head and pressing a soft kiss directly in the middle.

"This is the site of your injury, yes?" he asks, resting his cheek on it.

Nodding, I attempt to swallow, but the sight of this beautiful man being gentle and loving with a part of my body I'm used to hiding has left my throat completely dry. "It's not pretty, I know."

"It is though," he says confidently. "This here," he traces the length of my scar from top to bottom, "represents an event in which your life could have ended. Easily. But it did not." He presses a kiss to the very top of the scar and moves down, each little suckle leaving me shaking with need. "You are with me now because of how strong you are, Harper. This scar represents your resilience, and there is nothing more beautiful to me than the strength that glows from deep within you."

"Come here." The words come out in a ragged whimper as I reach for him.

He takes my hand and pulls me close, maneuvering our bodies until we're on our sides—me on my right, and him behind me. He pulls down the front of his shorts, and his cock springs free. I steal a glance at it over my shoulder, and I can feel my cheeks growing hot at the sight. It's wide and long, with a thick mushroom head and veins running along the length of it.

Luka lifts my shirt enough to reach between my legs and pushes two fingers into my core. I clench around them as I claw at the twisted heap of sheets in front of me. We've made a mess of this bed, and I still need more.

My hips jerk against his hand as his tongue traces the shell of my ear. "You are already so wet for me, *ledai*," he says in a husky voice that makes me wetter.

"Yes," I cry out, but before he can hook his fingers inside me to make me come, I stop him. "Wait, let me get something." Reaching over to my nightstand, I pull out my vibrator.

"What is that?" Luka asks.

In response, I turn it on. His eyes widen at the vibrating sound. Then I hand it to him. "Hold that against my clit, and you'll have me screaming in seconds."

His gaze narrows on the toy, and I wonder if the suggestion to use it offends him.

"Are you...okay with this?"

He pulls my back against his chest and presses a kiss against my hair. "I was just picturing you screaming as you come unraveled in my arms. I am more than okay with anything that helps turn that exquisite vision into a reality."

He carefully lifts my leg and drapes it over his as he gets into position. Lovingly caressing my hip, he asks if I'm comfortable as he presses a kiss to my neck.

"Yes," I moan, spreading my dripping folds for him.

He drives into my pussy with one fluid motion, stealing my breath. I wrap my fingers around one of the thin copper bars of my headboard just as he presses the vibrating toy against my clit. My back arches away from him, but he holds me steady as he pumps into me from behind.

"Oh god. Oh god," I shout as my thighs start to shake. My body feels like a bowstring about to snap.

"You feel so good, Harper," he grunts into the crook of my neck. His hand slips beneath my shirt to my breast, squeezing the soft flesh until my nipple hardens against his palm. "Mmm," he moans when he feels the skin tighten there. He plucks at it once, twice, and the sensations are so overwhelming that I grab the pillow beneath my head and scream into it.

The third time he rolls my nipple between his fingers, I'm thrown off the edge and into the abyss. I think I scream his name, but I can't be sure because my body is floating and combusting into a ball of flames all at once.

His teeth sink into my shoulder blade as he roars his release seconds later. We lay there for a long time, our chests heaving and our bodies still connected, until Luka pulls out and goes to the adjoining bathroom to clean up. When he returns, he pulls the covers over both of us and pulls me into his arms once again, my back to his front.

The next day, I wake to him watching me with a smug grin on his face.

"What's the smirk about?" I ask, lightly shoving against the wall of his chest.

He pushes a lock of hair behind my ear, then runs his fingers along my cheek, lips, and chin. "The sight of you sleeping so peacefully, your lips swollen and your hair a mess...I am solely responsible for your disheveled state."

I let out a giggle while rolling my eyes. "Wow. Such a dude comment."

He pulls me toward him until my cheek is pressed against his heart. "Do not dismiss the pride I am feeling," he says with a laugh before shoving his nose into my hair.

We spend the morning lounging in bed for a bit longer before we shower together and get ready for the day. He helps me give Viper his medications, mostly by keeping a foot of distance between them while I do it.

It's early afternoon when we take a cab to his apartment since it's closer to the church than mine. The brothers are all home and having a wonderful time watching *Seinfeld* reruns, if their constant riotous laughter is any indication. We kick our shoes off by the door and join them on the couch.

At one point, Mylo takes the flip phone out of his pocket to show me all the new ringtones he bought. He has the theme songs for each of his favorite shows, all assigned to his brothers. He's particularly excited about the *Seinfeld* ringtone, which he's assigned to Kyan, because Kyan reminds him of George, as he is "equally selfish and unpleasant to be around."

It takes me a full episode before I realize this must be the first time they've ever seen it. That's when I stop watching the show and start watching them instead. Particularly Luka.

There's something wholesome about witnessing someone you love watch something you love for the first time. Your emotions are still so fresh in your memory that when they experience those feelings in front of your eyes, you feel them too, even though the content in front of you is not new.

It's like–

Wait, I *love* him?

Love isn't something I ever expected to feel again. After my divorce, of course I hoped to fall in love again someday, but I wasn't counting on it.

I don't know when it happened, or how it could've happened so quickly, but when the word floats through my mind again, it feels like it belongs there.

I love him.

When he gets off the couch to grab something from the kitchen, I don't even notice he's returned until he stands in front of me with a plate in his hand and an expectant look on his face. "Harper?"

"Sorry," I say, my voice distant and dreamy even to my own ears. "What?"

"Would you like some kooky cookies?"

He removes the aluminum foil covering the dish to reveal a pile of oatmeal cookies.

"What did you call them?" I ask, certain I must've heard wrong.

"Kooky cookies. Talia made them. They are delicious."

Shrugging at the odd name, I grab two. I stifle a moan after the first bite but can't hold it back after the second. "These are so fucking good."

Mylo laughs. "They are indeed."

The plate is empty by the time it's passed around to all the brothers. I feel myself sink deeper into the plush cushions of the couch for two more episodes, then my eyes drift to the clock on the wall.

"Shit! We're going to be late," I stammer as I get to my feet. "Luka, we have to go."

"Oh, yes, right," he says, his hands drifting to my hips before pulling me against him. "Late, late, late, we would not want that, now would we?" He nips at my neck, and I become very aware of the four sets of eyes on us.

"Right, well, good hang today, boys," I say, pulling on my jacket and shoving my feet into my boots.

I don't pay attention to who says what, but I hear them call out, "Have fun," "Enjoy your evening," and "Farewell, Harper." The fourth brother doesn't say anything. He just giggles, and that brother is Zev.

It isn't until we're halfway to the church that I realize how weird I feel. My steps are slower, and I know that because it feels like I'm trudging through sand, even though it's a concrete sidewalk. Luka jogs ahead of me to get a closer look at a wall of posters featuring a turtle on top of a pile of toilet paper rolls. He points at it, laughs so hard that he clutches his chest, then runs back to tell me about it.

"Do you see this?" he asks, still laughing.

"Yeah, I see it," I reply, wondering what's so funny about it.

When the wall starts to look like a Magic Eye painting and I edge closer to find the hidden image, panic sets in.

"Shit. Luka, how many cookies did you have?"

He's still too busy laughing at the turtle to look at me, but he holds up a hand with all five fingers outstretched.

Jesus Christ. I only had two, and I'm absolutely flying.

My pulse quickens. "Luka," I shout, tugging on his arm, "you need to call Talia or Jay and find out what was in those cookies."

His laughter settles into a soft chuckle by the time Jay picks up, which I'm grateful for. "What is in the cookies Talia made for us?"

I can't tell what Jay's saying at first, but then I hear, "Bro, why do you think she calls them kooky cookies?"

"Fucking hell!" I shout.

Luka hangs up with Jay and rubs his hands up and down my arms. "Harper, all will be well. It appears there are," his face scrunches up as if he's bracing for my wrath, "drugs in the cookies, but we shall endure this night together. I will not let anything happen to you while we remain on the kookies," he promises, dragging out the pronunciation to become "koooooo-kies."

"You mean the kooky cookies?"

He furrows his brow. "That is what I said."

"No, you don't understand," I tell him, jerking out of his grasp. "My parents have never seen me drunk. I didn't even drink at my brother's wedding because they were there. They can't see me high off my ass."

"I do not have parents, so I am not following," Luka says casually as he sits in the middle of the sidewalk. "What is the worst that could happen if they see you floating on the kooooo-kies?" Then his eyes cross as he leans back on his hands and repeats, "koo-kies, kookies, kookies."

"My friends in high school all had curfews, but I wasn't even allowed to leave the house on a school night. If I didn't get straight As, I'd be grounded for weeks, meanwhile, my brother coasted through all of his classes, and he could do whatever he wanted."

I start pacing in a small circle around Luka, mostly because pacing is my go-to move when I'm stressed, but also because creating a circle shape with my feet feels good. It's like I'm weaving a cocoon around Luka where he'll be safe from my parents' judgment. Because if they find out not only am I high on weed cookies but that my boyfriend gave them to me, I'm worried my dad will strangle him in front of a bunch of dressed-up children.

Maybe I don't need to be worried at all. We can just skip the play and go home. Sure, my parents will be disappointed, but far less than they would be if we stay.

"Luka, let's go. Let's just get out of here," I tell him, urging him to get up.

He slowly and clumsily climbs to his feet. I notice a patch of dirt on the back of his jacket and go to brush it off when I hear, "Harper, there you are."

My heart sinks.

Mom is all smiles as she strides toward us, her arm looped through my dad's. Her long brown hair is swept into a neat updo with subtle stripes of silver at her temples. She's wearing a long dark-red skirt belted at the waist with a black button-down silk blouse beneath her matching black peacoat. My dad is wearing one of two blazers he's owned for the last two decades, pleated gray khakis, and white New Balance sneakers.

"Well, look at this. You've brought a friend," my mom says, eyeing Luka as she extends her hand.

"Hello, kind humans," he mutters.

When he goes to reach for her hand, he misses and swipes at the air once more before I grab his arm and pull him against me. "This is Luka. He works long hours as a private bodyguard. He's a bit tired today."

My dad grunts, and I feel my lips form a frown. That's his disapproving grunt. I'd know it anywhere.

"Well, shall we get in there?" I suggest, gesturing for my parents to take the lead.

Mom nods but stops before they take another step. "Harper, what on Earth is wrong with you?"

Shit, can she tell? I feel like I've been so careful. "What do you mean?"

Her eyes drop to my left hand, and I realize I've been thumping my cane on the ground for no reason.

"Oh, just, um, getting ready for the orchestra," I say with a laugh. "You know how much I love...drums." I don't love drums. I mean, they're okay, but I've never been particularly interested in them.

"Honey, it's a third-grade play. There's no orchestra."

Right. I clutch my cane in one hand and Luka's massive bicep in the other as I silently pray for a miracle.

The lights are already out when we enter, but Luka and I only stumble once before we settle into our seats next to my brother, Derek, and his wife, Faith. The curtains part, and I let out a sharp gasp at the sight of the humongous, half-built snowman in the middle of the stage. He's wearing a scarf and has a pipe and button nose, but the children running around the stage through the fake snow have yet to give him his eyes made of coal.

He can't see without his coal eyes. Why haven't they given him his eyes?

Derek leans over and whispers, "Don't worry, sis. You don't have to take any of the kids home. They all have parents already."

I elbow him in the chest, maybe a little too hard, and he groans as he folds at the waist. Faith rubs his back but is too focused on Nathan, her son, rolling a fake snowball in his small hands to pay too much attention.

"What kind of creature is that?" Luka asks, chuckling softly as he stares at Frosty's unfinished body.

My mind latches onto the idea that Frosty doesn't come alive without his eyes and top hat, making me wonder if he has any level of consciousness before they put those on. Is it like he's in a coma? Can he hear distant voices, but can't see anything? Or is he fully aware of everything around him and exists in a desperate, voiceless state until a child decides to give him a hat?

What if there's a soul inside that body of snow? And what happens to it when the snow melts?

"No, no, no," I mumble as I climb over Luka's lap, then my father's, then my mother's, to reach the aisle. I race up the wide steps and into the hallway. I can't find the restrooms, so I lean my head against the brick wall next to the water fountain. Turning the water off and on has a calming effect, so I keep doing it.

Suddenly, my focus is broken when my brother approaches, offering me a slow clap. "Wow. I must say," he puts a hand over his heart, "I am beyond proud."

I turn off the fountain, but I don't meet his gaze. "What the hell do you mean by that?"

"You are so fucking high."

"Bullshit."

He shuffles closer in an annoying, dance-y way, then in a quiet voice, says, "Whatever it is, I want some." He holds his hand out, and I look from it to his bulging brown eyes, back down to his palm.

"I don't know what you're talking about."

"Oh, come on. It's so obvious. You're losing your shit in there while your boyfriend is riding the chuckle truck." He holds his hand out again, and I shrug. "Ugh, how am I supposed to get through this play completely sober? It's not like the kids know any of their lines."

"Aw, your life is so hard," I say, mocking him. "You refuse to put any effort into what you do, even fatherhood, and yet you still come out looking like a prince."

Derek rolls his eyes. "Jesus, this again? Mom and Dad still not giving you enough praise? How is that my fault?"

"You know what?" I bark out. "It's not. Let's just go back in there."

I hear a "tsk" from my mom when I struggle to climb back into my seat, but I ignore it and keep my head down for the next several minutes. Maybe if I don't look at the stage, I won't have any more of those unsettling existential thoughts about a fictional snowman.

Glancing at Luka, I notice he's watching the play intently while chewing on the collar of his puffy jacket, and I'm relieved that he seems to be having a better time than I am.

When I hear Nathan's sweet, angelic voice, I make the mistake of looking up as he throws a fake snowball at one of the other kids, and once again, my attention drifts to Frosty. He's wearing his hat and his eyes are in place, which comforts me at first. But then, it looks as if Frosty turns his head to look at me. I look away, shielding my eyes with my hand.

Luka notices and reaches for my other hand, bringing it to his lips. He kisses each fingertip, then starts gently chewing on my middle finger, just as he had on his jacket collar.

I can't bring myself to address that though, because a high-pitched voice says, "Harper? Harper, help me. I don't want to melt."

No, no, no. This isn't happening.

"Harper," the voice calls out again, "Harper, don't let them take my hat. My hat is like my beating heart. Don't let them rip my hat from me, Harper!"

"I can't help you," I whisper back, sending out a silent plea for him to leave me alone.

"What was that, my mate?" Luka asks, leaning over to me.

"Nothing. Nothing."

As long as I don't look at him, the voice will stop talking to me.

"Harper," the voice says again, this time, angrier. "Do not ignore me, Harper."

It continues harassing me. Calling my name over and over until it feels like it's shouting directly in my ear. I can't take it anymore, so I jump to my feet and shout, "Leave his hat on or he'll die!"

When every pair of eyes in the room lands on me, Frosty stills. He goes back to being an inanimate stage prop rather than the lost soul trapped in a pile of snow I thought he was.

Shame threatens to send me to my knees, but before that happens, I yell, "Sorry," and walk as fast as I can up the steps, and I don't stop until I'm out of the building.

It doesn't take long for Luka to catch up to me, and to his credit, he doesn't try to comfort me. There's nothing he could say right now to make me feel better. The most frustrating part is that I know once I'm on the other side of this high, I'll feel worse. So it's only going to get shittier from here.

We hail a cab two blocks from the church and clumsily undress once we get back to my place before climbing into bed. He presses a kiss to my forehead and says, "All will be well, *ledai*," and I fall asleep convinced that everything is broken, and that's how it'll stay forever.

I wake to the sound of my phone vibrating across my nightstand. It continues until it falls over the edge, and I scramble to get it without toppling out of bed. Swallowing the enormous lump in my throat, I answer. "Hi, Mom. Listen, about last night."

I don't pick up all the words she yells, but the important ones certainly stick:

"Disgusting display."

"Traumatized children."

"Praying for you."

"Boyfriend or dealer?"

And the grand finale: "Never more disappointed."

"Mom, I'm so sorry," I tell her. "It was just a really unfortunate miscommunication."

"Do you need rehab?" she shouts. "Because we can't afford to send you to rehab, and I bet you can't afford it either after your divorce."

"Mom," I say, scrubbing a hand down my face. "I don't need rehab. I promise you."

She tells me she can't discuss this anymore and hangs up.

I stare at the phone in my hand until Luka's strong arms wrap around me, and before I can turn around to bury my face against his chest, my eyes fill with tears.

"Come here," he murmurs, lifting me in his arms as if I'm no heavier than a piece of paper and draping me over his lap. "I know you are hurting, but I am here, and I am not at all disappointed in you."

The image of him chewing on my finger pops into my head and I burst out laughing. "Thank you," I tell him, wiping the wetness from my cheeks. "So, how did you feel last night?"

He huffs a breath. "That was quite an experience. I must say I enjoyed it immensely. That is, until I saw how distraught you were."

"Yeah, I, uh," I stammer, embarrassed to admit it, "I thought Frosty was alive and that the kids would kill him if he melted or lost his hat."

"The rounded snow creature wearing the scarf?"

"Yep."

He rubs the scruff of his beard, mulling over my words. Then he curls a finger beneath my chin and lifts until his lips hover just above mine. "That must have been terrifying for you. But I am not surprised. Your soft heart moves you to save anyone or anything that needs saving. Even if that thing is a lifeless heap of artificial snow."

Luka kisses me, and it's tender in all the ways I need it to be. The moment he pulls away, my tears resume falling, and the next words out of my mouth are, "I love you."

His mouth falls open, stunned, I'm sure. I wait patiently for him to say something, anything, but he doesn't.

Instead, his hands fly to his face, and he begins aggressively rubbing his eyes.

"Luka? What is it?" I ask, concern pooling in my belly as I try to pull his hands away. "Let me see."

He's much stronger than I am, and my attempts to push his hands aside are futile.

"Ahh," he moans in pain as he continues rubbing, now using his nails to scratch at the delicate skin of his eyelids.

"Should I call 911? Luka, tell me what's happening."

I flip my phone open and press the first two numbers when, out of the corner of my eye, I see his hands drop to his sides. When he turns to look at me, his eyes are red, but not the pinkish color that comes with rubbing the skin. This red is bright, blood-red, and it's where the whites of his eyes should be.

"Oh my god, Luka," I scream, my hands on either side of his face. "Your eyes are wicked red right now. Talk to me. What's going on? Has this ever happened before?" He says nothing, so I tell him, "I'm calling an ambulance." I grab my phone again to press the final number, but he yanks the phone from my hand and throws it against the wall. The several pieces that were once my phone skid across the floor. When I turn to face him, I don't recognize the man in front of me. "What the fuck? Why?"

"Do. Not. Call. The authorities," he says through gritted teeth. The veins of his neck are popping out, and his eyes still look like they're filled with blood.

I don't know what to do. "I–I wasn't," I stammer, holding up my hands. His focus on me, albeit menacing, allows me to look closely at his eyes though, and I notice the iris and the pupil are untouched. The red color is restricted to where the white should be.

When the red color starts to blink, reminding me of a turn signal on a car, I freak the fuck out.

"It…it's blinking. Your eyes–they're flashing now. Wh-what do I do?" I plead with him, trying to reach for him, but he jerks away as if my very touch would burn him. "Tell me what to do."

"It is nothing," he finally says. "I am fine."

"You are not fine," I shout. Moving slowly, because I have no idea how to make Luka feel calm, I sit on the edge of the bed. "Luka, whatever it is, we can deal with it together, okay? You and me." I plaster on what I hope is a warm smile. "We're a team."

He paces around my bedroom like a caged animal, but when he hears me say we're a team, he freezes in place. His shoulders lower, and he finally looks somewhat calm. Maybe now he'll listen to reason. "Where's your phone?" I ask, looking around the room. "I don't think we need to call 911, but we should still make an appointment at the nearest Urgent Care."

"No!" he roars. The little hairs on the back of my neck stand at frightened attention. "My eyes are no business of yours. Leave it alone."

"I'm just trying to help you," I yell back, my anger rising at the realization that just moments ago, I told Luka I loved him. He never said it back, and now he's screaming at me because I'm worried about him. "What do you want from me?"

Luka's hands ball into fists at his sides. "I am not some helpless animal that requires your rescue, Harper. Just leave me be."

His words slice through my torso like a knife. "I never said..." Before I continue begging him to see this situation from my point of view, I decide I've had enough. This day started out spectacularly shitty with the call from my mom, and now I'm getting berated by the man I love for expressing concern. "You know what? Fine!" I shout, releasing all my fury from the tip of my tongue. "Get the fuck out then."

He looks like he's been slapped, but the blinking has stopped, and the red has faded back to white. Luka's eyes are normal again. Why bother even pointing it out to make him feel better? He doesn't want my support.

"Very well," he mutters quietly. He picks up his clothes and doesn't say another word as he stomps downstairs and slams the front door behind him.

# CHAPTER 15

## LUKA

*M*y body aches with the need to return to my mate. Every step I take around the city is pure agony. It has been only a few hours, and I feel as if I have been separated from her for decades. My loving, precious mate. I now know for certain that is what she is. My mind in this form never doubted it for a second, and while my draxilio hungered for Harper in a lustful sense, the two of us were not aligned on whether we could spend eternity by her side.

That is, until Harper's heart broke while on the phone with her mother this morning. Hearing her mother scream such hurtful words that would leave the deepest wounds in Harper's psyche wrecked me. Harper's tears after the phone call ended were even worse.

It was not the same as when Colin hurt her. The emotions that followed felt natural. The rage and intense desire to destroy him for the pain he caused. That I could do, and I knew I would never regret doing it.

But this? There was nothing I could do to remedy this pain. This was a disagreement between my mate and her mother. I could do nothing but offer her the comfort of my arms and the reassurance that she was still a wonderful, selfless creature deserving of love.

Incredibly, it worked. She giggled at my words and let me hold her until her tears stopped falling. Then she said she loved me, and my draxilio's eyes were finally opened. I felt the realization click into place as he registered her vulnerable state, the devotion that pumped through his veins to protect her from even the slightest discomfort, the tiniest twinge of sadness, until his very last breath.

I did not even get the chance to tell her that I love her too. Of course I love her. She is the reason I left my home planet and traveled through space to get here. She is the center of my universe. I was not able to say any of that before my eyes started itching to the point of pain, then turned red. Immediately, I lost myself in a cloud of paranoia believing I was on the verge of losing her.

Harper was trying to care for me. She was trying to get me the medical attention she thought I needed, but I could not hear it. I could not even breathe as I pictured her look of disgust the moment she learned of the monster I truly am. Or the image of my brothers strapped to steel tables as they are poked at and studied in a hidden laboratory much like the one we spent our childhood in.

I also knew that the sudden redness of my eyes was a result of the genetic modifications my brothers and I were given. Our handlers said that genetically modified draxilios—podlings—did not have mates, that they did not exist at all for us, but I was always suspicious of this. Even with the impressive ways they were able to alter our cellular makeup, how could they possibly control *that?*

When podlings started to go missing, a rumor spread throughout the laboratory that our handlers found another way to keep us tethered to our roles as living science experiments. Our eyes turning red in the presence of our fated mate was a way to signal that our focus was no longer on our main duty—serving as the king's assassins—and a lack of devotion to our king meant they could no longer control us. They tried everything they could to intervene, but since they failed to develop a potion or surgical technique to break the mate bond, if our eyes turned red, we would be sentenced to death. It was not known to the public that podlings were sentenced to death after their eyes turned red, but we knew. Together, we mourned the brothers and sisters we lost.

We came to Earth to avoid that fate, and the sight of Harper reaching for the phone to contact the authorities took me back to Sufoi and the endless torture my brothers and I endured.

It was not my intention to scare her or to raise my voice in her presence, but when she insisted on taking me to see a doctor a second time, my fears consumed me, and she was the unfortunate recipient of my distress.

I do not know what to do.

My draxilio growls angrily. *Find our mate. Make it right.*

I want what he wants, but I do not know how to make it right without revealing the truth about me. There is no way for her to become my mate officially until she knows the truth, but what do I say? How do I ensure that she will not be terrified at the sight of my horns or my blue skin? Will she even forgive me after the way I behaved?

I know she has a new phone because she sent me three digital messages checking to see if I am okay. Even now, the flip phone in my hand feels like it will shatter beneath my grip, but I cannot seem to put it down on the chance Harper attempts to contact me again.

If she does, I am not sure I will have the words she deserves to hear. Because telling her the truth about what I am means putting my brothers at risk. When we came here, I did not realize I would be thrust into this position. Foolishly, I assumed it would be easier than this, but love is not easy, not for humans, anyway. There is no sense of certainty for them when it comes to love.

Ahead of me, a male hands a wrapped bundle of fresh flowers to a delighted female. She takes the flowers and presses them to the tip of her nose, breathing in, then clutches them gently to her chest before pressing a kiss to the man's lips. The scene moves me in a way I was not expecting.

Humans stumble through their pitifully short lives having to trust that the one they vow to cherish for eternity will not cause them harm. I have gained a profound level of respect for how fearlessly humans leap into love. They have no guarantee that a net will appear below and catch them, and yet they continue to leap.

I must do the same, I realize. Harper leaped when she told me she loved me, and she was rewarded with an intimate look at my wrath. My behavior was despicable, and if she is ever to forgive me, I must take the biggest leap possible.

The sun has set by the time I leave the flower shop. The biggest bouquet I could find fills my arms as I pause on the sidewalk to hail a cab the way Harper showed me. Once inside, I direct the driver to take me to her home. She plans to meet Ryan at the clinic tonight to teach him the surgical techniques Dr. Brooks refuses to give him access to, but I am hoping she has not left yet.

"Harper," I shout as I knock on the door. "It is Luka." A whiff of her fear scent reaches my nose, and I cannot tell if it is new, or from earlier when I yelled at her.

When there is no response, I knock again, three times, so that she can be certain it is me.

"I am sorry, Harper," I yell through the door. "I–I would like to speak with you so that I may repair what I broke earlier today."

A muscle ticks in my jaw as Harper's fear scent gets stronger. If she is home, why would she be afraid?

*Him.* Colin's face pops into my head as my draxilio growls incessantly. There is something disturbing happening behind this door, and I am certain Colin is the cause.

I curse under my breath at my inability to effectively influence him to leave her alone. When he showed up at Harper's clinic, I was barely able to control my rage. That is not an emotion I have experienced while trying to influence someone. It took the entirety of my focus to keep from shifting into my draxilio, and as such, my influence on Colin when I threatened him was weak. Now he has my mate.

Dropping the flowers to the ground, I pull out my phone and send a message to Axil.

> Colin has Harper. Need your help.

I do not wait for him to respond. The front door splinters into kindling when I kick it down, my mask falling away as my pale skin fades into my natural, rich cerulean. My heart skips a beat when Harper's shape comes into focus.

As I step across the threshold, I realize she is barely clinging to consciousness, her head lolling to the side as blood streams down her face from a wound on her forehead. Her mouth is gagged, and her hands are tied behind her back.

In front of her stands Colin, and I watch in horror as he backhands my mate across the face, knocking her chair over onto her left side and holding a long, double-barreled gun less than an inch from her face.

# CHAPTER 16

## HARPER

*P*ain. Blinding lights. Something wet running down my nose. More pain. I remain locked in a cycle of waking long enough to register that several spots on my body are throbbing to an excruciating degree, but before I can figure out where I am or what the hell is going on, blackness fills my vision and I'm pulled away again.

"Hey!" someone shouts, and my eyes flutter open.

My vision starts to clear, and the blurry gray blob with a black top in front of me turns into Colin. He's wearing a black beanie and a light gray jumpsuit with a zipper that stops at the base of his throat. The look on his face is the most frightening thing I've ever seen. He's smiling, but behind his eyes, there is nothing, just an empty void where normal human emotions should be.

Letting out a muffled cry through the fabric stuffed in my mouth, I try to move, but my hands are trapped behind me, tied together with what feels like rope.

Colin leans forward, resting his hands on the edge of my kitchen table, which is covered in a layer of newspapers with several weapons lined up across them.

How did this happen? How did I get here?

I search my memories for a clue as to what could've led to this moment. More importantly, where the fuck is my bodyguard? Wasn't he supposed to prevent this very thing from happening?

Scattered images flash through my mind, and Luka's blood-red eyes bring it all back. His eyes turned red, we both lost our shit, got into an argument, then he left. Trying to distract myself from the searing pain of my broken heart, I went out and bought a new phone. Even though I should've continued punishing Luka with my silence, I sent him a few texts, checking on him.

He never responded, so I texted Ryan to see if he could meet me at the clinic early to get started on the secret training session.

But I never even left my house. I took a shower, changed into my scrubs, and when I came downstairs, I remember hearing a floor-board creak seconds before a damp cloth was pressed against my mouth.

"Are you awake or what?" Colin shouts, kicking my chair. The jarring movement brings the pain to the forefront of my mind, and then I feel all the places on my body that are cut, bruised, or broken.

Tears spill onto my cheeks, and he laughs maniacally. "You know, this could've been avoided. If you had just accepted my apology and met me for a second date, none of this would be happening. You have only yourself to blame."

I can't talk because of the gag, but even if I could, I wouldn't have a clue what to say to that. There's nothing rational left in this man's head, so there's no point trying to explain how that statement is completely batshit.

"I shouldn't be surprised, really," Colin continues, running a hand over the shotgun at the end of the table. "Nice guys always finish last, right? It's a saying for a reason. No matter how nice I am to the women I date, none of you seem to appreciate it. I paid for your dinner," he shouts, slamming his fist into the table. "It's expected, so I fucking did it. I was happy to do it. Is it really so unreasonable to expect a little something in return? Something to show your appreciation for the nice gesture?"

*I used my cane to break your nose instead of your floppy pencil dick, so you're welcome,* I want to say. Instead, I continue to cry, hoping either Luka comes to save me, or Colin kills me in a way that isn't painful. At this point, that's all I have left to cling to.

"Men have to pay for dinner. That hasn't changed," Colin continues, "but nowadays, we have to ask first if we can kiss you, then respect your boundaries if you say no, then hope you'll give us another chance to go through the whole routine again. What about *our* needs?" he scoffs, grabbing the shotgun off the table and switching the safety off.

"This is my favorite gun," he mutters, stepping around the table to stand in front of me. "I never go hunting without it."

A knock on the door has both of us jerking our heads toward the sound. I can barely hear the words, but I know it's Luka. My heart leaps when he yells through the door to apologize for the fight we had, and I hope I get the chance to tell him all is forgiven.

My time is running out, that much is clear. Bile creeps up my throat as I struggle against the rope that binds my hands. I need more time, but how do I stall? If not for the gag, I could keep him talking, but I can't even do that, so I summon my few remaining tendrils of strength and channel it into my lungs as I wail into the gag, hoping Luka will hear me.

The back of Colin's hand slams into my cheek, the force of it knocking my chair over and sending my bad knee directly into the floor. My vision blurs as the pain explodes through my leg, up into my torso and into my skull.

As the edge of my vision fades to black, I notice a massive shape has burst through my front door. At first, it looks like Luka, then I notice the color of his skin is different. It's strange. Almost a bright blue, in fact. Two thick, black horns curl out of his head right at his hairline, ending in terrifyingly sharp points. Even like this, he's devastatingly beautiful. It hurts to look at him.

Or maybe that's just my knee that hurts.

None of this is real. It can't be. I have more than one head wound, and my eyes are playing tricks on me. I'm concussed, and this is a hallucination. *Yeah, that's all it is,* I tell myself as I drift into nothingness.

# CHAPTER 17

## LUKA

*Kill Colin. Save mate.*

Kill Colin. Save mate.

My draxilio and I are in total agreement on our plans for the evening as the thin slivers of wood that used to be Harper's door crunch beneath my feet. I do not bother masking my skin because I would like this to be the last thing Colin sees before I snuff the life out of him: a creature straight from his nightmares intent on making him suffer.

The moment he sees me, he points his gun toward my chest and pulls the trigger. The projectiles clatter to the floor after bouncing off my body. The mushy brain inside his head cannot make sense of this, causing him to loosen the hold on his pitiful weapon. I capitalize on his lack of focus, taking two strides to reach him, and I revel in the dread on his face when I snap his precious gun into three pieces and toss them behind me.

"Wait, no—" Colin mutters as I slam my fist into his right eye. His body immediately goes limp, and I catch it before tossing it onto the kitchen table. His weight topples the table with a loud crack, and his body crumples into an awkward heap atop his small collection of shiny toys.

Now that Colin is taken care of, temporarily anyway, I shift my attention to my mate. Racing to her side, I carefully remove the gag from between her lips and free her hands from the tightly knotted rope.

"How is she?" Axil asks behind me.

I sigh as I press my finger against her neck. "Alive, but her pulse is weak."

Axil kneels beside me, and I cradle her head as he helps me move her body into a less painful-looking position, but I am careful to not jostle her too much as I do not know the extent of her injuries. The sight of blood running down her face and the bruises already forming on her cheek and wrists feel like a knife buried deeply in my side.

My draxilio clamors to take over. He growls at me to let him out. *Kill him. Kill him. Kill him. Avenge our mate.*

*There is plenty of time for that later,* I send back. *Harper needs us now. She comes first.*

But it would not hurt to know the status of the weak male. "Kyan, is Colin dead? Check his pulse."

A moment later, Kyan hollers, "Alive, but not conscious."

I tell Axil to grab a clean cloth from the kitchen and soak it in water. He returns immediately, and I press the damp cloth to the wound that still bleeds on her forehead.

"She needs medical attention," I mutter as a deep sense of self-loathing fills my chest. "This is my fault."

"It is not, brother," Axil replies, trying to comfort me.

"Shall we kill him?" Zev asks from across the room.

"If you let him see you like that, we will need to," Kyan adds. "He knows too much and will certainly share what he knows with anyone who will listen."

He is right, and while my draxilio agrees, I cannot bring myself to care about the state of Colin when my mate barely clings to life in front of me.

I hear Mylo and Kyan exchanging their typical cutting barbs over what to do with Colin, and the clash of blade against blade follows shortly after. They are playing with Colin's daggers, no doubt.

"Wait," I hear Mylo mutter with a shushing sound. "Do you hear that?"

"What?" Kyan asks.

"It is like a scratching sound."

Peeling the cloth back from Harper's head, I am relieved to find the bleeding has stopped. "Get me more clean, wet cloths," I tell Axil.

"No, I hear nothing," Kyan finally replies to Mylo. Then they resume their dagger play.

I do not have the energy to scold them, so I pretend I do not hear them at all as I check the other wounds covering Harper's body.

"He is awake!" Mylo suddenly shouts. "Luka!"

I turn to see Colin on his feet, aiming a black pistol at my mate's head.

Mylo and Kyan rush toward Colin, but from the darkened staircase behind him, Viper leaps onto Colin's shoulder with a furious cry. Colin yelps as Viper drags his claws down the side of his face, causing Colin to fumble with the gun in his hand. With the intended damage done, Viper scampers away just as Colin's finger slips and pulls the trigger.

A loud popping sound fills the air as the gun goes off, and blood splatters across the wall behind him. Then his body folds in on itself as the contents of his skull spill onto the floor.

"Mmm—" Harper groans, and hope surges through my blood at the prospect of her survival.

Her eyes do not open, but her lips smack together as she slowly wakes.

"What do we do?" Zev asks, his voice thick with panic.

I want to forget Colin and focus on Harper, but I cannot ensure her recovery until I figure out what to do about Colin's corpse. It does not matter in which order we handle things; the authorities will come. They will investigate the scene and it does not look good for me and my brothers. We stand among a dead male and a wounded female, and even though we are not responsible for either, the fact that we are present does not bode well.

I do not know what will happen when the authorities arrive, but I do know that my brothers cannot be here when they do.

"Okay," I begin, gesturing for them to step closer. "Listen to me carefully. You will leave through the back door. You will shift in the alley, and you will fly back to the site where we crashed."

"But—" Axil tries to interject, but I keep going.

"You will not return to the city until I let you know that it is safe to do so. Do you understand?"

Their eyes remain locked on me, but they say nothing.

"Do you understand?" I repeat.

"Yes, brother," they reply in unison.

"What about you?" Zev asks me. "What if we do not hear from you?"

I put a hand on his shoulder and pull him into a hug. "I will handle whatever comes of this," I vow. Then I pull back to look at him, to look at all of them. "But if you do not hear from me, then you must fly west for at least a day before you land. Pick a new shade if you wish, but you will need to secure a new shelter and new identities. You will begin again."

"We cannot," Mylo protests.

"You can and you will."

Mylo looks as if he wants to argue but stays quiet.

"It will be easier next time. You know what to do, and you have ample funds to do it."

"I really must insist—" Axil says, holding up a hand, but I do not let him finish.

"Your mates are still out there," I remind them. "Mine is here, but yours are somewhere out there, waiting for you to find them. You will leave here, and you will not look back because your futures are with them. Not me."

I could not properly protect my mate. If she survives this, I will ensure that Colin's demise is in no way attached to her. I could not properly protect my brothers but making them leave the city might allow them the opportunity to grow into the strong, loyal males I know they can be.

My brothers reluctantly file out the back door, Axil at the back of the line. I grab his arm, and he whirls around to face me. "Watch over them."

He nods, pressing his fist over his heart. "I will."

The sound of the back door closing is the last thing I hear before the blare of approaching sirens fills the air.

I have failed every person I care about, but I can help them all right now. And I shall.

# CHAPTER 18

## HARPER

The fuck is that noise, and why is it so loud? I wake to a handful of different beeps, all coming from behind my head.

The beeps are forgotten the moment Luka's back comes into view just outside my room. He's talking to a cop, and though I can't immediately figure out why, I know it can't be good.

A nurse brushes past them and into my room and smiles brightly. "You're awake," she says, much too chipper for how much my head hurts. Then over her shoulder, "Ms. O'Connor is awake."

A doctor, another nurse, Luka, and the cop all rush in. Luka's hair is mussed and flat, the circles under his eyes darker than I've ever seen. He looks so weary, my poor bodyguard. Despite his rumpled appearance, the expression on his face is pure determination, and just beneath that is unwavering devotion.

I wish everyone else would just leave so I could lean against his hard chest and ask what the fuck is going on.

The doctor says something about stitches and a concussion and something, something, something about my knee. I don't really listen to any of it.

"Want some water?" the nurse asks, and I notice just how dry and scratchy my throat is. "Take small sips, okay?"

I nod, pressing my lips to the plastic edge and moaning when the cold liquid hits my tongue.

"Slow down," the nurse urges. "We don't want to upset your stomach."

When I empty the cup, she refills it and leaves the pitcher on the table beside me. "Press this button here if you need anything, got it?"

"We will, thank you," Luka says with a slight bow, causing the nurse to giggle nervously as she leaves.

Unbelievable. Even when he looks like he hasn't slept for days, he makes every woman around him blush.

He pulls a chair next to me and threads my fingers through his. I can tell he has a lot to tell me, but he stays quiet in front of the cop.

"Ms. O'Connor," the officer says, approaching the foot of the bed. "I'm sure you're in a great deal of pain right now, but I was hoping I could get your statement. Anything you can remember from before you ended up here. Mr. Monroe has given me his account of the events, but I'd like yours as well."

Taking a deep breath, I wince at the pain slicing through my left side, then curse under my breath as the cop waits patiently for me to stop.

"I remember," I mutter, desperately trying to pluck an image, a shape, something from earlier. Then I see him. Colin, and his hideous sneer as he blamed me for the blood streaming down my face. And the moment he backhanded me for attempting to scream.

Then...Luka.

Luka and his imposing frame after he kicked my door down. Luka, and the way his broad shoulders filled the doorway as he strode inside my house with his fists clenched. Luka, and his tall, proud horns.

Wait, what?

"I remember Colin berating me for not going out with him a second time."

The cop scribbles on his notepad, and as the memories flood back in, I spit them out.

"The first date we went on, he pulled me into a dark alley and tried to force himself on me." I don't realize I'm crying until Luka gently strokes a finger across my cheek, wiping them away. "He texted me repeatedly, he called, he sent me flowers, and when I refused to respond to all that, he showed up at my place of work, telling me I embarrassed him for not showing up on a date I never agreed to go on.

"I think he somehow broke into my house and attacked me from behind when I was in the living room."

The cop nods, then eventually tucks his notepad into his coat pocket. "Thank you, Ms. O'Connor. This is very helpful." He hands a card to Luka. "If you think of anything else, please don't hesitate to give us a call."

I wait until the cop's footsteps disappear down the hall, then squeeze Luka's hand. "Tell me everything."

A smile tugs at the corner of his lips. "Where would you like me to begin?"

Easy. "Your eyes. Start there."

He sighs heavily as he drops his head against the back of my hand. When his eyes meet mine again, they're filled with unshed tears. "I am not what you think I am, Harper. I am so very sorry. For everything. For the many ways I have failed you."

I don't make any suggestions or offer any theories as to what he is, though I do have one of my own. Instead, I let him sit in silence, waiting for him to say it.

"I am not human. I-I come from a planet called Sufoi, and I have the ability to shift between forms—the one you see before you, and a much larger creature. One who can fly and breathe fire."

Okay. I figured he wasn't human after his blood-red eyes started to blink. I definitely did not expect the rest. "You mean, like, a dragon?"

"Yes, though, on Sufoi, we are called draxilios."

He still hasn't answered my question. "Why did your eyes turn red?"

Luka explains how he and his brothers were genetically modified at birth, giving them unique traits and abilities compared to natural-born draxilios, and how their eyes turn red when they're faced with their mate.

"So I'm your mate?"

"Indeed you are," he says, kissing my knuckles. "I knew it from the first moment I saw you at that dance hall."

"The night you asked me to go home with you to fornicate?"

He laughs. "That was my failed attempt at seduction."

The memory makes me smile. "Definitely not your best work."

My gaze drifts down to the raw, blistered skin on my wrist, and suddenly I remember where I am. "Wait, what about Colin? What happened?"

Luka holds up his hands. "I take full credit for the bruised skin around his eye and any injuries he incurred when I threw him across the room. But I swear to you, I did not kill him."

"He's dead?"

"Quite."

"How?"

His brows lift in surprise. "I realize this will sound ludicrous, but if not for Viper, Colin might still be alive."

"Viper?" I laugh, not believing him for a second.

"Yes," he vows. "I was tending to you, and I tasked my brothers with watching Colin. He was unconscious, so it should have been a simple task. But they got distracted by Colin's knives, of course."

"Of course," I repeat with a chuckle. I can absolutely picture that.

Then he describes the harrowing moment Colin stood with a gun in his hand, and how the five dragon shifters watched as the three-legged cat attacked Colin, causing him to fumble with the gun and pull the trigger just as it pointed toward his chin.

In the end, it was the special-needs rescue cat, on the staircase, with the pistol.

I should feel guilty for even thinking of such a distasteful joke about the recently deceased, but since the recently deceased is Colin, a man who was planning to murder me, I absolutely do not.

"What does this mean for us?" I ask, wondering what it must've looked like when the cops arrived. "Where are your brothers?"

Luka winces at the mention of them. "I sent them away until this is…sorted out."

He pulls his chair closer to rest his chin on my arm. His eyes swirl with shame, guilt, and adoration, and I can't help but trace the hard line of his jaw.

"I do not know what this means for us, Harper," he says with a sigh. "An ability I have as part of my modifications is that I can influence the minds of humans. I did what I could to convince the cop I played no part in Colin's death. That I showed up in time to save you and to witness his accidental death, but I am not certain it was enough."

"What do you mean?"

"My grasp on human criminal investigations is tenuous. I do not understand their processes, nor do I know that the use of my power on the cop was enough to protect us from being blamed for his death."

He must see the fear in my eyes because he wraps his arms around me, carefully avoiding all my bruised parts, and presses a kiss to my cheek. "No matter what they think and what their investigation reveals, I will not let any of it impact you."

"Too fucking late," I tell him, my tone cold as I wiggle out of his grasp. "If it impacts you, it impacts me."

"You mean," his gray eyes sparkle with hope, "you and I are still a team?"

"I guess that depends," I say, pursing my lips. "Is there anything else you'd like to tell me?"

He stares at me blankly for a second before it clicks. Then he scoots out of his chair and kneels on the floor beside me. "Earth is a much harsher place than I expected. I thought it would be easy to blend in with humans though it has been anything but," he says with a sigh. "Then I met you. Harper, you dim the harsh, blinding light of this world to a soft, warm glow. I can see this world clearly with you at my side." He presses a kiss to my palm. "My heart is yours, Dr. O'Connor. Now and for the rest of time."

Sniffling, I nod and add, "I love you too."

# CHAPTER 19

## LUKA

*H*arper is released from the hospital two days later. She has a bruised rib, three stitches in her forehead, and several scrapes, blisters, and bruises, all of which make my draxilio growl at the sight. Her knee is swollen and bruised, but she did not suffer any additional fractures, which I am grateful for.

She reluctantly lets me carry her up to my apartment where most of her clothes and her beauty products already are. Viper is also here, and his purr is deafening when I tuck Harper into bed next to him. The same bed he has claimed as his own ever since I packed up his things and brought him here the day after Colin's death.

Bouquets of fresh flowers cover every surface of my bedroom with heartfelt notes from Ryan, Eliza, Harper's brother, and her parents, wishing her a speedy recovery.

We do not know what will happen next, but the one thing Harper is certain of is that she never wants to step foot in her townhouse again. Not that she could right now even if she wanted to. It is still a crime scene, according to the authorities, but even once the investigation is over, she said she could never feel safe there. We have discussed leaving the city entirely, an idea that I am very much in favor of. It is too crowded for me. I cannot shift as often as I would like, and I am ready to leave the vile memories of this place behind us.

My brothers have not returned, and I am glad about it. The apartment feels empty without their constant laughter and bickering, but it is also nice to be alone with my mate.

The next day, Harper grows restless, outright refusing to stay in bed to let me wait on her. She wishes to visit the clinic and check on the status of her patients. Dr. Brooks has been covering for her, but she does not trust his ability to offer her patients the same care.

I tell her I will only take her to the clinic if she uses the crutches the doctor sent her home with, and she pouts for several minutes but eventually agrees.

I give the address to our driver, a private driver I hired to take us where we need to go until I learn how to drive on my own, and we arrive in seven minutes. She lets me help her out of the car, and a squeal of excitement fills the hallway the moment we enter through the back door. Eliza charges toward Harper, but skids to a stop when I step in front of my mate to block her path. "Careful. She is in a great deal of pain."

Eliza nods. When I step aside to reveal Harper, she shouts, "You're here! We've missed you so much. How are you feeling?"

Ryan finds us shortly after, and Harper updates both of them on the status of her injuries.

I follow my mate to the little office she shares with the owner of the clinic, who lets out a sigh of relief upon seeing her. "You're back. Thank god."

"Well, not officially, but I wanted to see if there's anything I can help you with until I'm ready to start seeing patients again."

Dr. Brooks frowns, crossing his arms over his chest. "Well, how much longer are you going to be out?" His voice is a sharp whine, with every word sounding more and more irritating the longer he speaks. "I already had to cancel my trip to Virginia Beach this weekend. I can't keep covering for you."

Harper drops the chart in her hands, letting it land on the floor with a soft whoosh. She stares at him, and I smile as I watch her. I can tell from the way she stands and the defiant glare in her eyes that her next words will not be ones Dr. Brooks will enjoy hearing. "Hire someone else then."

"Excuse me?" Dr. Brooks asks.

Harper's spine straightens just a bit more, her confidence growing with each passing moment. "Yeah, you know what? I quit."

The doctor scoffs, an incredulous look on his face. "You're not quitting."

"Oh, yes the fuck I am, *Paul*." Her tone is biting when she utters his first name. "You're really going to give me a hard time for calling in sick after being kidnapped and beaten? Find yourself a new doctor."

She leaves the office and I follow close behind. Dr. Brooks follows too, but I whirl on him and hold his gaze until he cowers. He does not take another step in her direction. She catches Ryan and Eliza on her way out, letting them know what happened, that she has plans to open her own clinic, and that they will have a place there. They hug her gently and tell her to call them as soon as she is ready.

When we arrive home, Harper settles on the couch and opens the new laptop I bought her. She starts searching for homes for sale, trying to determine where we should settle. We have yet to complete the mate bond, but I am patient. Her body needs to heal, and I will wait as long as it takes for that to happen. She is already my mate in every way that matters.

I turn on the TV, and I hear Harper suck in a breath when a picture of Colin's face pops up on the screen. The news anchor relays the facts of the case, but I hear nothing over the rapid beat of my heart and the ringing in my ears. The buzz of the doorbell is a welcome interruption, but only until I open the door to find the officer who took our statements standing there.

I let him in, and Harper quickly turns off the TV before he steps into the living room. "Ms. O'Connor, it's good to see you on your feet."

Harper nods as she leans on her crutches, her bottom lip disappearing beneath her blunt teeth.

"Well, I won't take up much of your time, I just wanted to let you know the status of the investigation dealing with Mr. Colin White," he begins, and I can tell from across the room that Harper's holding her breath, just as I am. "It turns out, there is no Colin White. That was one of three names he had fake IDs for. He worked as a temp at the company listed on his social media for two days before he was fired. His legal name was Scott Sheffield, and he was wanted in Nevada for multiple sexual assault charges.

"As for the night of your attack, Ms. O'Connor, we were hoping the security cameras outside the real estate office across the street and on your neighbor's front porch would provide clarity on the events," he adds, and my throat feels as if it is starting to close.

"Cameras?" I ask, trying to hide the shakiness in my voice. If there were cameras pointed at Harper's front door the night of the attack, then the moment I unmasked my skin after kicking the door down would have been captured. The cops would be able to see my true form.

"Unfortunately, the footage from that night seems to be missing from all feeds," the cop says.

I silently thank all the gods in the universe for this stroke of luck.

"But we were able to confirm that the guns were registered to Mr. Sheffield, and the blood splatter on the wall aligned with the description you provided, Mr. Monroe, of when the gun accidentally went off."

"What about Gidget?" Harper asks, her voice filled with worry.

"Uh, Gidget?" the cop asks, looking back through his notes.

"He had a dog named Gidget," she explains. "A two-year-old white Bichon. The last time I saw her, she was sick. Did you find her at his house?"

I have to stifle a chuckle. My mate and I are waiting to receive confirmation that our lives will not be significantly derailed by Colin's death, and she is concerned about the fate of his dog. I could not love her more if I tried.

"Ah, yes," the cop says. "The dog is his mother's. He was living in her basement, and as far as we can tell, she had no knowledge of what he was doing or the outstanding warrants in Nevada."

"Okay, great. Good to know," Harper mumbles. "That's it then? This whole thing is just...over?"

"Yes," he replies, closing his notepad. "We have a clear picture of what happened that night, so there's no need for further investigation."

The cop thanks us for our time and then leaves. I lift her into my arms the moment the door closes and hold her flush against my body. We stay like this for quite some time, just listening to each other breathe, with the knowledge that nothing else stands in the way of starting our life together.

My fingers tangle in her hair as I bend down and kiss her deeply, allowing the kiss to communicate all the ways in which I love her, and how that love will never fade.

She pulls back to look at me, her wicked smile sending a rush of blood to my cock. "Time to claim your mate, you beast."

Viper hisses when he hears the growl in my throat and scurries out of the bedroom. I kick the door shut behind me and finally claim my mate.

# EPILOGUE

## HARPER

TWO MONTHS LATER...

"$\mathscr{E}$asy with the dresser, guys," I call out, gritting my teeth as Mylo and Kyan hold it above their heads as they carry it through the narrow hallway of our new home. I shield my eyes from the early afternoon sun blasting through the floor-to-ceiling windows.

Despite the bright sun in my eyes, I can't help but smile as I watch my handsome husband and his brothers move our belongings into the house I fell in love with the moment I saw it listed. It's a gorgeous colonial-style home in Salem, New Hampshire, with a brick exterior, four bedrooms, three bathrooms, close to an acre of land on either side, and a private fenced-in patio where Luka has room to shift.

Just a ten-minute drive down the street from our house is where the vacant commercial building I bought is almost done being painted and will soon house several painfully expensive machines that will help me care for my patients in the best way I know how. Eliza and Ryan have moved into a two-bedroom apartment just off Main Street, and Luka and I are paying their full-time wages as they help me get the clinic up and running.

Once the whole messy business with Colin was behind us, I learned more about Luka's "special power" and how he used it to swindle hedge fund managers and investment bankers out of their cash, expensive watches, and their entire annual spending budgets. I have no idea what happened to those guys once Luka convinced them to transfer money to him, and I can't bring myself to care very much. Especially when we donate large amounts of that money to local animal shelters. It's a much better use of the money than the finance bros snorting it up their noses.

"You look happy, *ledai*," Luka whispers against my neck as he wraps his arms around me. "Are you?"

I now know that *ledai* means my heart and it doesn't matter how many times he says it, the word never fails to make me melt. I've also learned that "*joshik*" is the name of an insect on Sufoi with a pathetically short lifespan. When these bugs hatch, they consume the waste of other bugs as well as their own, and then die two days later due to their poor diet. So when Luka calls someone a *joshik*, it's truly one of the harsher insults I've ever heard.

Placing Luka's hands over the part of my belly that's currently growing a half-alien baby, I sigh against him. "I am indeed. Blissfully happy, in fact."

"Did you send Talia a new bump photo?" he asks.

"Shit, I forgot. Will you take one?"

He nods as he pulls out his phone, and I turn to the side with a wide smile on my face. "Beautiful," he says as he types something on his phone and presses send.

Two weeks after I got out of the hospital, Jay and Talia packed their bags and moved to Colorado. They're in the process of opening their bakery and are patiently waiting for the day Talia can legally add her kooky cookies to the menu.

They were sad to miss our wedding, but truthfully, we probably wouldn't have invited them anyway. Our wedding was small but everything I wanted. Because I wanted to be able to see Luka in his natural state on the day I pledged forever to him, Luka's brothers were our

only guests. Mylo was ordained via the internet and served as our offi-
ciant. The ceremony was under five minutes, and the six of us ate and
danced and drank until the sun came up.

My parents weren't pleased to learn they didn't make the guest list,
but it was more important for Luka to be unmasked on our wedding
day than for my parents and brother to be present. Plus, our relationship is still strained after my little weed-fueled outburst at Nathan's
play.

I apologized to them once again and to Nathan and his teacher. I
also sent a large donation of books and school supplies to his school
the following week, but it still doesn't seem like enough for my mom.
I'm not sure it ever will be, and that's okay. I've come to accept that I
don't have to strive for her approval. She's entitled to her feelings, and
so am I.

At this moment, I can honestly say I've never been happier. I have
my own family, and like the little creature in my stomach, it'll continue
to grow.

"Pizza is here," Zev calls out, holding a stack of boxes in one hand.

"How many pizzas are you planning to eat on your own?" I ask
him once we crowd around the marble kitchen island. "Because I'm
eating for two, so I'm gonna need at least one of these."

Mylo and Kyan bicker over the only Hawaiian pizza, and I catch
Luka rolling his eyes as he watches them.

Viper meows as he scampers around the kitchen, hoping for a piece
of crust to hit the floor.

"When are you moving into your new house?" Luka asks his
brothers between bites. "Have you met any of the neighbors?"

"The bedrooms are almost finished," Axil replies. "It is on a beautiful stretch of land in Sudbury, and we did meet one of the neighbors.
She is a kind old woman named Franny."

"Lady Norton," Mylo corrects. "She prefers to be called Lady
Norton."

"No, she does not," Kyan says. "That is merely what you wish to
call her."

Mylo drops a piece of crust onto the floor for Viper as he stares daggers at Kyan. When his gaze shifts to the rest of us, his expression softens. "She gave me this book. Something about a Bridgerton. I forget what it is called. Anyway, the characters in the book have fancy titles like that, and when I called her Lady Norton, she requested I never call her anything else." He turns back to Kyan. "So that is her name."

"Speaking of books," Mylo continues, "I have an idea. We really need to study other aspects of human culture beyond TV. There are endless books, movies, documentaries, and something called reality TV that we have yet to explore."

Mylo practically bounces in place as he describes his plan while the rest of them roll their eyes, quietly groan, or avoid making eye contact with him as he speaks. "The best way to accomplish this is to divide each type of media between us, then meet once a month to discuss our learnings."

"You are serious?" Axil asks, looking as if he'd rather suck a brick than participate.

"Yes, I am serious. This is the best way I have found to learn their interests, the shifts in their culture, and the slang they use." Mylo slams his empty cup on the counter to get their attention. "We studied human history before we came here, and that taught us nothing."

"Apart from their penchant for buckles," Kyan adds with a mocking grin.

"If we truly want to blend in with the humans, this is how we do it."

"Fine," Axil eventually groans. "Though I have no interest in mingling with any more humans." His gaze settles on Luka. "Not after what you and Harper went through. I plan to focus on my wood-working and avoid all females."

"You plan to avoid all females?" Mylo asks with a scoff. "What about your mate?"

"If she is out there," Axil begins, putting a heavy emphasis on the word *if*, "she and I will cross paths, but until that happens, I will not risk my eyes turning red in front of a human."

Zev and Kyan voice their agreement with Axil's plan. Mylo, however, stays quiet.

Something tells me he's going to break several hearts with his newfound love of literature.

Luka clears his throat. "What you need is to get jobs. Find what inspires you, what interests you, then turn it into a trade."

The brothers stare at him blankly.

"Whatever you choose to do, stay out of trouble," Luka adds, clear warning in his tone. "I am not leaving my mate and child to drive up to Sudbury to bail you out of jail. I will not do it."

"Do not worry, brother," Axil says, clapping a hand on Luka's shoulder. "I will not let them get into any trouble."

"Zev will not have a difficult time finding a trade, will he?" Kyan says, giving Zev a nudge with his elbow.

"What are you talking about?" Luka asks.

Zev's cheeks turn pink as he quietly says, "I can manipulate machines."

"What?" I shout, my voice a high-pitched shriek. "Since when?"

Kyan smiles wickedly. "Since he erased the security camera footage of you entering Harper's home unmasked the night Colin died."

"You did that?" Luka asks, his mouth gaping as he stares at Zev. "I thought you were out of the city. I told you to leave until the investigation was complete."

"And you thought we would listen?" Axil says with a playful scoff. "You are family, and you needed us."

Luka's gaze lands on me, and I know what he's thinking. He can't believe his brothers disobeyed him, and he's tempted to scold them for it, but he ultimately won't because they proved they aren't just prone to fuckups after all. In fact, they might be able to take care of themselves.

After we finish eating, it takes the guys another hour to finish moving our stuff into the house. They wrap me in bear hug after bear hug as they wish me well and tell the child in my belly that he or she has four loving uncles eager to meet them. Axil pulls me aside as the guys put on their coats and tells me to close my eyes and hold out my hands.

When I open my eyes, I let out an audible gasp. "You made this for me?"

He nods proudly as I gaze down at my new cane. "The handgrip is a cushioned dragon head," he says as he traces the shape with his finger. "Then there are flames etched into the shaft, which is made from cedar."

I'm in awe as I look over the intricate designs. It's absolutely gorgeous, as is the base of the cane, which is shaped like a spiked dragon tail.

I give Axil another tight hug before they pile into Axil's new truck, and Luka and I watch from the gravel driveway until their brake lights disappear.

Then I follow Luka into the garage where he pops the hood of our new car so he can stare at it. Again. He doesn't know how to drive, but he loves looking at all the intertwined parts beneath the hood as if it's some mysterious puzzle he needs to solve.

"I can take you out tomorrow, if you want," I suggest, resting my head against his bicep.

"You will teach me?"

"Of course I will." When his eyes light up with excitement, I say, "Do you want to get in now, and I can show you how to park?"

He considers this for a moment but ultimately declines. "You should rest, *ledai*. Would you like me to rub your knee?"

As fun as that sounds, I have other plans. I shake my head as I grab Luka's hand and tug him toward the patio.

Once we step into the center, he chuckles. "Again?"

"Yes, again."

"I am surprised you have not grown tired of this, *ledai*."

I scoff. "We need to make up for lost time, okay? You could've been giving me dragon rides for months, but you kept your identity a secret. And I get it, really, but that doesn't make me want one any less."

He shakes out his arms and legs as I step back about four feet to give him space. "Where would you like to fly tonight?"

"Maybe over Boston?" I suggest. "I love the peace and quiet here, but I do miss the city lights sometimes."

Luka shifts into his draxilio and purrs loudly as I pat the large tip of his nose. He opens his claws, and I wrap my coat tighter around myself as I crawl inside and sit, crossing my legs. My stomach drops when Luka launches himself into the air. Wind whips through his claws the higher he gets in the sky, and I peek my head out from between two claws so I can watch the ground speed by below.

I drop my hand to my belly as I sit in awe at the incredible view that stretches as far as the eye can see. This is all that matters, right here. My child, my dragon, and me.

* * *

Thank you for reading HER ALIEN BODYGUARD! I hope you loved Luka and Harper's story. Are you wondering what happened when the brothers moved into their new house? And Axil's pledge to avoid women at all costs? Good news! You're about to find out!

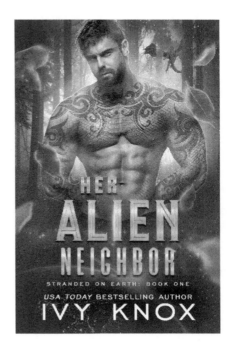

Start reading HER ALIEN NEIGHBOR now!

# ALSO FROM IVY

# ENJOY THIS BOOK?

Did you enjoy this book? If so, please leave a review! It helps others find my work.

Get all the deets on new releases, bonus chapters, teasers, and giveaways by signing up for my newsletter.

# FROM IVY

This prequel was not the first book written in the series. But once I finished Axil's book, I couldn't wait to go back in time to 2007 when the brothers first crashed and see them struggle to blend in with humans in Boston. It ended up being just as much fun as I anticipated. From the outfits of the late aughts, to the music, to the flip phones, I loved revisiting all the trends.

Luka had me swooning immediately. He's always been the leader of the group, but beyond that, I didn't know how he would end up on the page. He's a tough disciplinarian, but that's because he has to be. His brothers would expose what they really are in a second if left to their own devices. So Luka keeps them in line and uses his powers to ensure they're fed, clothed, and sheltered. But, of course, this creates an issue when he's trying to spend time with Harper because he can't be in two places at once. In the end, he was softer and much more empathetic than I originally envisioned, and I loved that about him.

Then there's Harper. She's fantastic and strong and very easy to love, but my favorite thing about Harper is her bite. She has that signature Boston, no-BS approach to life that might seem like it doesn't fit with a sunny, positive attitude, but it just makes you love her all the more. She expects the best but reacts accordingly when the worst occurs.

I wanted to include more of the banter between the boys and Aunt Franny, a.k.a. Lady Norton, from book one, but it felt like this story needed to end when Luka and his brothers go their separate ways.

And last, but not least, there's Viper—the true hero of the story. Picturing Luka, a massive alien dragon shifter, having to tiptoe around his own house to keep a three-legged cat from hissing was just hilarious, and he felt like the perfect way to bring Luka and Harper together despite the cat's desire to keep them apart. There was also something deeply satisfying about Viper being the one responsible for a trophy hunter's death.

Next up, we flash forward to present day, where Axil is about to fall in love with the girl next door.

Stay tuned!

Love,

Ivy

P.S. - Without my amazing editorial team: Tina, Chrisandra, Mel, and Jenny, this book would just be a heaping pile of crap. They work hard to help me turn my messes into heartwarming happily ever afters. I'd be lost without them.

# RESOURCES

SAMHSA (Substance Abuse and Mental Health Services
Administration Hotline)
1-800-662-HELP (4357)
TTY: 1-800-487-4889
samhsa.gov

RAINN (Rape, Abuse, & Incest National Network)
1-800-656-4673 (call or chat)
rainn.org

National Suicide Prevention Hotline
1-800-273-8255 (call or chat)
suicideprevention.org

National Domestic Violence Hotline
1-800-799-SAFE (7233) (call or chat)
thehotline.org

# ABOUT THE AUTHOR

Ivy Knox has always been a voracious reader of romance novels, but quickly found her home in sci-fi romance because life on Earth can be kind of a drag. When she's not lost on faraway worlds created by her favorite authors, she's creating her own.

Ivy lives with her husband and two neurotic (but very cute) dogs in the Midwest. When she's not reading or writing, she's probably watching *Our Flag Means Death*, *Bridgerton*, *New Girl*, or *What We Do in the Shadows* for the millionth time.

Printed in Great Britain
by Amazon

45710876R00090